GEORGE MACKAY BROWN

Andrina

And Other Stories

TRIAD
GRAFTON BOOKS

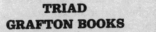

LONDON GLASGOW
TORONTO SYDNEY AUCKLAND

Triad
Grafton Books
8 Grafton Street, London W1X 3LA

Published by Triad/Panther Books 1984
Reprinted 1990

Triad Paperbacks Ltd is an imprint of
Chatto, Bodley Head & Jonathan Cape Ltd and
Grafton Books, a Division of the Collins Publishing Group

First published in Great Britain by
Chatto & Windus/The Hogarth Press 1983

Copyright © George Mackay Brown 1983

ISBN 0-586-05991-1

Printed and bound in Great Britain by
Collins, Glasgow

Set in Ehrhardt

to JOHN L. BROOM

Acknowledgements

Acknowledgements are made for stories already printed or broadcast as follows: 'Michael Surfax, Whaler': *New England Review* and the *Scotsman*; 'A Winter Legend': BBC; 'An Epiphany Tale': *Scottish Field*; 'The Chamber of Poetry: *Rhythm of the Glass* (Paul Harris Publishing); 'A Candle for Milk and Grass': *Glasgow Herald*; 'The Box of Fish': the *Scotsman*; 'Poets': BBC; 'King and Shepherd: *Brunton's Miscellany*; 'Andrina': the *Scottish Review*, BBC; 'The Feast at Paplay': *Scottish Short Stories* (William Collins); 'The Day of the Ox': *New Edinburgh Review*; 'The Lost Boy': the *Scotsman*; 'Darkness and Light': the *Scotsman*.

CONTENTS

MICHAEL SURFAX, WHALER

The whale rose lazily, as if to get a better view of the horizon. The harpoons in its flank, the two boats full of men, it seemed quite unaware of. Another harpoon, flung by Isbister, skidded off its gleaming hide and raised a little silver fountain from the sea. From far away, a thin voice came shivering over the water: 'Put about . . .! Come back . . .!'

The whale seemed to hear this voice. It turned for a second or two from its reading of the horizon, and it seemed to Bronsky at the tiller of the first boat that a light of understanding broke across the vast blunt forehead. Then it plunged. Two hundred tons of salt water hit the *Fergus* and the *Odins*. The *Fergus* was overwhelmed. Wallace, who was on his feet, braced and ready to cast another harpoon, was flung in an arc athwart the sudden surging hill of water. The others were swamped. From the *Odins* could be seen heads bobbing among whirls of green water and chunks of ice.

'I told you, come back!' came the insect voice from another world.

The *Odins* survived the massive onset. Only Leask was thrown out, and never seen again. The five other boatmen were flung upon each other, a tangled web of flesh, leather, hair, iron. At last, in the shuddering boat, they managed to disentangle themselves. Marwick the bow-man had a red-flowing wrist wound from someone's harpoon.

By the time it occurred to them that shipmates were drowning and freezing in the sea, it was too late. Not an arm or head was to be seen. The *Fergus* turned slowly, upside down, as if it too was seeking, blindly, the six who had manned her.

The voice came again, flawed, across the sea of whale-fare and drowning. The skipper of the whaling ship was beside himself with rage and anxiety. The five survivors in the *Odins* could not piece together the urgent words: even if they had cared to.

'The old bastard!' said Isbister. 'It was him that launched us against the whale. A foolish order – a piece of criminality. And because we have had a lean trip. This monster whale was to make up for everything. Them in their grand houses, in the town of Dundee, the whale-masters, they would be pleased – they would pay Surfax a bonus. Not a penny for the likes of you and me. And for that hellish nonsense, seven men are drowned!'

The others in the *Odins* said nothing.

Meantime the great whale, as if indeed it had glimpsed some good thing under the horizon, a mate or a legion of plankton-locating birds, was surging rapidly into the east. It was possessed by a huge pulse, the sea fell away from the beast in white throbbing furrows. (Or perhaps it was the tickle of the harpoons that had stung it into a splendid rage.) It sundered the ocean where it fell, and fell, and fell.

How could they have ever thought to see such magnificence plumbed for oil, sawed and salted into steaks, its head made a network of bones for some museum in Dundee or Glasgow?

'You bloody crazy old fool!' Isbister cried in the direction of the whaling ship, towards which the *Odins* edged now with hesitant striking oars.

Macpherson did not row. His head was down on his saturated knees, his shoulders were convulsed.

'Now, Isbister,' said Marwick, 'now, man, there's been overmuch trouble this voyage. We volunteered to man the boats. That's the truth. Be glad you're alive!'

The Highlandman sobbed, over and over again, 'I have lost him that I loved better than hawk or horse. He is drowned. He is lost indeed, forever.'

By this time they were close enough to read the name *Swede*

Boy on the whaler's prow, and (when they swung their heads round) to fix on the intent white face at the rail.

The quiet horizon, miles off, quivered like a struck string. Their quarry had broken through the line. It was gone.

Michael Surfax, skipper of the *Swede Boy*, whaler out of Dundee, said (and his voice, close by, was dull as pewter now), 'I ordered you, not once but four times, to turn back.'

'It was too late,' said Marwick, shipping his oar.

'Did it not occur to you,' said Mr Surfax, 'to take the *Fergus* in tow? What are you thinking of? She is undamaged, as far as I can see.'

There was silence for a full minute between the whaler and the whaler's boat; except for Macpherson, who said, 'Seven brothers I had, none dearer than him!' And his blunt fingers across his eyes glittered with other water than what dripped from the oars.

Isbister said, in a voice of complete awe, 'Turn round then. We are to fix a line on the *Fergus*. Mr Surfax has said it.'

When they were half-way back to the upturned *Fergus*, Marwick saw a dark swan-neck arch out the green water. It was followed by an unrecognizable blur – a grey mask between frozen hair and frozen beard. The mask uttered a few distinct syllables of pain or wonderment; then the half-ghost was dragged under again by the weight of water in its clothes and boots.

Marwick's oar yearned towards the slight broken swirl.

Isbister said, 'We are sent not to pick up corpses, but to fetch the *Fergus* back. Mr Surfax ordered that.'

Between the Faroes and Shetland Michael Surfax wrote, with considerable fluency, several letters in his cabin.

[1]

'To Sir Malcolm McPhallin-Gray, merchant, in the port of Dundee, Scotland.

'Dear Sir, the *Swede Boy* has had, thus far, but a moderate trip. We stalked whales between Greenland and Newfoundland, to no avail. Iceland waters yielded us two, but one old and diseased, that I thought better to abandon. I have had the usual stirrings and murmurings from the crew, mainly (as has happened before) on account of the food, but they can see plain enough that I eat the same food as themselves. There is one Orkneyman, Isbister, that will not sail with me again. We struck a fine beast two days after midsummer, in golden waters. The flensing knives were sharp, we turned that sea red, barrels bulged at the end of the day. Then, for a week, nothing. "Has every whale in the sea," I asked at the supper table, "gone to an assembly of whales off Spitzbergen?" The length of the board, not a man laughed. I think it my duty to give them a cheerful countenance, it leavens somewhat their labours and discontents.

'Then, sir, into my glass next morning swam this king of whales, a Behemoth, larger than any my eyes had ever beheld. I balanced prudence with daring. If we struck him, and held him, and wore him out, it would be the most famous cargo of whale ever to enter the port of Dundee. I knew that I, and my men, would share in the overplus of profit, but I reasoned more that it would be a shining honour to your family and firm and whaling-fleet. Two boats, *Odins* and *Fergus*, manned with volunteers, were sent against the huge placid sea-dome. (Sir, the creature seemed marked for death; ready, passive, and acquiescent.) The first harpoons were flung, and they adhered. Still the whale seemed asleep. The two boats circled her closer. I saw then what I dreaded, for I had seen it before, always as a prelude to disaster. The creature seemed to heave up, and hang, as if it had drawn a vast breath. I cried through the trumpet of my hands, again and again, for the boats to return. They heard me, surely, but the lust of blood and money was on them. They drew closer, more barbs were flung. Then the whale subsided, with a mighty displacement of water, wherein, I regret to say, *Fergus* was swamped, with the loss of all hands. But later I contrived to recover the boat, virtually undamaged. *Odins* somehow rode the wave, and suffered the loss of one man only, William Leask. We did not attempt any pursuit of the whale, being grieved by the loss of so many fine men. The knowledge that their lives were adequately insured, upon their signing on, must prove some satisfaction. We have fading hopes of another strike before the end of summer. Joshua Wharton of the *Reprieve*, whose path crossed with *Swede Boy* three days since, assured me there is a school, and many unattached whales, hereabouts. I live in hope. But the men are very wretched, some of them ill with scabs and complaints of the stomach, and speak only of Hamnavoe and home. The man Isbister I spoke of, the Chartist, I had to isolate below deck; where he still lies, darkling, and promises nothing in the way of obedience, loyalty, and honest labour. . . .'

[2]

'To Mistress Maria Leask, in Clouston, Stenness, in the Orkneys.

'Your man is dead. I will not soften the blow. I think he said once to me he had five young children at home. It is pitiable in the extreme. William Leask died with credit to further the comfort and well-being of his family. He died in front of an enormous whale, that not Samson nor Hercules could have subdued. Six young men besides were lost that same hour. Be assured, Mistress Leask, for your loss you will have as much money as ever you have seen. My intention is to come and see you, poor woman, in Stenness, as soon as *Swede Boy* anchors in Hamnavoe harbour. . . .'

[3]

'To the Russian consul in Leith, Scotland.

'Sir, A young Pole from the port of Danzig, by name Joseph Bronsky, is cast away on a whaling voyage near the coast of Greenland. The body was not recovered. Have the charity, I beg of you, to acquaint his relatives. Some monies owing to the deceased will be forwarded to them, along with his sea chest. . . .'

[4]

'Dear Williamina, how I am to put this letter together, is a matter of anguish and confusion to me. I cannot conceive how it will affect you, who must read it. The one of us is dead and drowned, and that one not I. How came it, my dear woman, that all of last winter and spring you would not or could not choose between him and me, and even on the day of our setting sail from Hamnavoe, your eye went uncertainly between us, full of pain and love. In moments of common sense I would say to myself, "Why, Michael Surfax, you are old, your beard is grey-flecked – you must not think a fine young woman like Williamina would prefer you to Laurie, who is as handsome and heart-winning a lad as ever the parish of Sandwick put forth. No, Michael, but I think she loves you just a little now because you are a man of reputation, a man with a command and money, a rock in the uncertainties of life. It will not last, Michael. She is a young beautiful woman. Laurie is Laurie. You, Michael, are but a step or two from tombstone and skull. . . ." But then I would reason, that a woman's heart does not feed on common sense. Perhaps, after all, the dice would come down in my favour, and in the end Laurie would have to look elsewhere for a bride. The goodness and innocence of the boy! The week before the departure of the whalers from Hamnavoe, he arrives at my cabin door, shy and smiling. "Mr

Surfax," says he, "please take me on this one voyage with you, if you can. I am much in love with a girl in Hamnavoe, I want to marry her before Yule. But I am a poor man. She can't still make up her mind. If I were to return from the Arctic with a little pouch of gold and silver, perhaps the precious coins would be a kind of shadowy sign of the love I feel for her. Please let me make my mark in your book. . . ." This Laurie said, standing just inside my cabin door. He could not know anything of the storm he had set raging in my breast. My immediate impulse was to say, "No, Sinclair, my crew was completed yesterday. I am busy. The *Swede Boy* sails in four days. Goodbye. . . ." Instead I told him to come back in an hour. He was back in fifty minutes, a faint smell of rum on his breath. "Why, Sinclair," I said, "you're a lucky man. It seems there's room for another crewman after all. Be here seven o'clock sharp in the morning. Get your gear together at once. No time for farewells. The woman will keep, if she's any good. . . ." Laurie nearly wrung my hand off, with relief and gratitude.

'Williamina, I am telling you all this, exactly as it happened. It is your due. Also, I wish to have the situation as clear as possible in my own mind, and writing (I have found) is a purifying fire.

'Laurie proved a good whaleman. He was liked by all our ship's company. He worked well and cheerfully. I had no fault to find with the lad.

'It proved to be, however, only a middling season.

'When, on the fifth day of July, a vast whale was sighted near Greenland, I was certain that, if the boats were to be launched, Laurie must be set in charge of one, he being a young man of resource and daring. I took him aside. I said, "Now, Sinclair, it's no good playing around with a whale like that. Go right up to her, put the harpoons in, then wait for the whale-storm to blow itself out. There'll be enough bounty money in it to buy a whole harem of brides." Our young friend smiled. He followed his five comrades into the *Fergus*, that soon bristled with harpoons.

'Whaling is a game of dice. Whalemen must take chances, or they starve. In this case they – Laurie also, as well as myself – underestimated the cunning and resource of the beast. It lay against them, it drowned seven of the twelve in a vast wave. Laurie was not seen again.

'Love too is a game of dice. But when there is only one player, how can he lose? I am half-a-year older since last I saw you, my dear. I have a heart greatly troubled. I need you now, if never before. Time runs out, but my love has not wasted by a single grain. . . .'

[5]

. . . 'In honesty I should tell you, it had been a hundred times better if Albert and Tom had bidden at home with you on the croft of Troddle. They were but poor hands at the whaling. Albert and Tom were in a small boat that was overset by a whale. Men die instantly in such intensities of ice. In due course, you will get guineas in accordance with the insurance pledged. Many an Orkney woman has anxious summers – year after year – till the whaling fleet returns. Keep your remaining boys at home. They are safer with ploughs than with harpoons, be assured. You may watch the corn patch growing, from now on, in peace.'

A WINTER LEGEND

The princess was a prisoner for fifty-one years in the high tower. Yet she did not grow older by a wrinkle or a gray hair from the first day of her imprisonment.

She did not know what became of her brother, the prince. He had been taken that same day, in the palace garden, by the soldiers, and dragged away crying through the tall gate.

'The king and the queen are both dead,' said a strange stern woman to the princess as she led her that day up three hundred and sixty-five circling steps to the high tower. 'A council of gray men rules the land now'.

The woman with the key said, 'Eat these worms and grass-blades – they're all you're getting to eat. Eat them, or you'll die. . . .' As soon as the wardress had gone away, the princess looked at the long cold worms and pieces of shrivelled grass on the plate. She was almost sick with horror. She pushed the plate away from her.

The wardress came back just before it grew dark. She said, 'I see you haven't eaten your good dinner. There's no more food for you until you eat the worms and the grass.'

Then she said, 'The sun's down. It'll soon be dark. Don't think you're going to get a lamp or a candle. You aren't. No blanket either. You must sleep on the cold floor. The council has given orders.'

The wardress lingered by the door. 'The council,' she said, 'has had pity on your sick brother. He has a job in the palace garden, helping the twelve gardeners. He carries water up from the river. He brings dung from the stables. He's so slow and weak the head gardener has to beat him every now and then. The head gardener is a strong bad-tempered man.'

The princess said nothing. She was glad it was dark, so that her torturer couldn't see her tears.

'Perhaps,' said the evil voice in the dark shadow of the door, 'you'd like to know what happened to your father and mother, the former king and queen? I'll tell you, they were drowned in the sea. Huge stones were tied to their necks and feet, and they were lowered out of a boat. They were sunk with all their finery on them.'

At that the princess wept. Her sobs echoed through the cold high cell. The wardress laughed – it seemed she liked the music of grief. Then, with a shrieking of hinges and locks, she closed the door of the tower.

The princess wept for a long time, until she had no more tears left.

When she lifted her head from her knees, she saw that a new moon was shining through the narrow slit of window; it brimmed the cell with silver light.

The princess was very tired; no wonder, after the turmoil and horror of the day just past. 'How can I sleep, though, in a cold place like this without a blanket?' Her maid Isabel always, every night, had brought to her bedside a little plate of sweets. Now, heavy with sleep, oblivious, she stretched out her hand and put into her mouth what was on the plate at her side, and ate it. She startled awake with a cry – she had swallowed the worms and the grass! Horrors! Yet her mouth and throat were all sweetness, as though she had sipped honey and wine.

The princess lay down. 'I might as well *try* to sleep.' The stones of the floor were warm, as though they remembered an age of sun-soaking in the royal quarry. They accepted the soft flesh of the princess as kindly as rose petals.

The princess thought, on the edge of sleep, 'How strange, the moon should have vanished an hour ago from the window. It's still there. . . .' Enchanted with sorrow and moonlight, the princess fell asleep.

Day after day, month after month, year after year, the princess lived in the tower like an unfading flower in a pot. The same things happened over and over. The same wardress came about noon with a plate of worms and grass; she said a few hurtful things to the girl and went away again. The princess had nothing to while away the time: no book or harp or embroidery frame. She tried to remember the stories her nurse had told her in her childhood, and found to her joy that she could remember them all: all except one, a winter legend that was a white confusion in her mind. Without those stories she might have withered. Not only did she tell them to the spider in the corner of her cell; she set them to music, she sang them to the blackbird or the thrush that came from time to time and perched on the narrow window ledge, cocking a bright eye at her. After she had sung a story, the bird sometimes would answer with a pattern of immaculate pure thrilling sound. 'Oh,' cried the princess then, 'thank you, bird. I wish I could sing as sweetly as that!'

Sometimes, when her throat was dry with recitation or song, the princess would try to picture the people in this story and that: their faces, their clothes, their gestures and movements. Then, behind her closed eyes, the story became a slow wonderful wordless dance, a masque. Each story had its own quite different ballet. Once she tried to remember the forgotten winter story; it remained a cold confusion; but when she opened her eyes she saw that a white butterfly had come in through the window and was drifting from wall to wall of her cell. She tried to take the butterfly in her fingers but it rose, fluttered, drifted out again. She cried a little; the butterfly was a more beautiful dancer than the dancers who moved through her ballets. 'Perhaps it'll come again, and stay with me for a while.'

Those dancing people in the stories – she tried to fix them so that they wouldn't drift and fade. She chipped a piece of stone from the wall one day. She scratched the childhood stories on the stone floor: the lion, the full moon, the witch, the fish-girl, the boy with the silver penny, the dragon, the simpleton, the wounded soldier, the frog, the apple-tree, the talking statue, the chimney-sweep, the seal-king. She had always been good at drawing (so her drawing master had said in the old days) but never had she drawn as well as she did now in the loneliness of her cell. Every single line that she scratched indicated something singular or important about the character, and how he or she stood in relation to the other characters within the circle of the story. . . . The princess was making of her prison a magic cave.

Months merged into years. The princess thought certain things were very strange in this place. For example, it had been a summer day when she had been dragged here and locked in; it remained summer; every day the golden finger of the sun wrote at the same level across the wall; there was never a day that a bee or a rose-petal didn't come drifting in through the high narrow slit of window; the bright eye and song of the bird never failed either. What had become of spring and autumn and winter?

And she never got dirty. Every morning in the palace she had been bathed and scented by her ladies. She knew that people got dirty; she had seen the thin hungry unwashed faces from the city slums at the palace gate before the guardsmen rode at them with lances and scattered them. 'The poor are dirty,' she thought, 'because they live far away from fountains. . . .' No water was ever brought to her prison. Yet when she looked at her hands, her legs, her sides, they were as lustrous as if she had just stepped out of the river. Sometimes she touched her face (for she had no mirror). Her fingers could detect no flaw or etching of time. 'Perhaps,' thought the princess, 'the dew comes in and clusters about me while I'm asleep.'

Yet, as the months and the years passed, she saw the deepening nets of age on the wardress's face and hands. The creature would stand wheezing for a long while in the cell door before putting down the daily plate of worms and grass-blades. Now she had not enough breath to hurt the princess with evil news; she could only squinny and sneer, and turn, and go away grumbling. The wardress was growing old, she was slowly breaking up.

One thing the princess *did* notice – her clothes were wearing out. She looked one day, and there was a hole in the elbow of her blue silk gown. With kneeling on the floor drawing with stone upon stone her stockings had gapes in them at the knees. Here and there were shreddings and unstitchings. The dust of the long long summer was working itself into the fabric; her dress hung on her, a soiled frayed thing.

In the old royal days she had seen the moon rounding out to the full, and then shrinking, and then vanishing into the House of Darkness. In this cell, at night, the moon never darkened. Always, over her sleep, the silver mask stood guard at the high narrow window: a gondolier, a fat smiling Chinaman, an old woman over fading cinders. The scratched stories on the stone were washed with moon enchantment.

How many years passed? The princess reckoned that fifty-one years must have passed since that guardsman had put the hood over her head and tied her hands behind her. If she had no calendar to tell her the exact count of time, her clothes said a little. They hung from her in tatters; the blue had long faded into a dull gray. They were so filthy they seemed only to sully her firm fragrant flesh. 'Perhaps soon,' she said, 'I'll have to live naked in this place!'

Next morning, she heard a wheezing and a choking in the

corridor outside her cell. The key screeched in the lock. The door opened. The shrivelled wardress stood there with her plate of sweet-tasting worms and luscious grass-blades.

'If you please,' said the princess, 'could I have a needle and thread to darn my clothes?'

Five minutes passed before the old one could find breath to speak. Meantime a leaf drifted in through the window; the princess noticed, astonished, that it wasn't a summer leaf, it was yellow and brittle.

The old woman said in a voice like a rusty knife, 'Needles, thread.... Your next dress, milady, will be your shroud. Worms and grass to eat – you should have been a skeleton long ago! Why are you not out of your mind with loneliness and heart-break? It's too bad, too bad.... Well, you slut, make the most of this feast. You're getting no more. Winter's here. I'll never climb that stair again!'

The old woman put a white mad look on the princess. Then she turned, the key shrieked in the lock; the girl heard her feet fumbling uncertainly down the darkling stair.

Never had the princess experienced such a night of intense cold and darkness. The long summer was over at last. The stone floor on which she lay, unblanketed, was drained of its long-stored sun. The masked moon had gone at last from the station at the window-slit. Winter, a black bony hand, clutched at her heart; her clothes were hardly more substantial than spiders' webs.

She endured the longest coldest most miserable night of her life.

Dawn came with a single snowflake; it undulated, a gray moth, past her window. Then the flakes came in a flurry and a flock; at last in dense ceaseless driven hordes.

As the princess watched, a lost snowflake came hovering into her cell. She had not seen snow for fifty-one years. She reached up on tiptoe, to grasp it before it drifted on to the floor and died.

She had it in her fingers. She opened her hand. It lay there, a fragile silver key!

The princess fitted the key into the rusty lock of her cell. It turned with a little silver sound. The door creaked open.

The stone stair spiralled down, twelve turnings and three hundred and sixty-five steps. As she went down the last web-thin rags fell from her in the dark airs that moved everywhere in the tower.

She would never never go back to that cell, now that winter had got into it. She would rather suffer the insults and gross looks of the guardsmen in the barracks-yard outside. A white glimmer, she walked along a corridor towards the great outer door of the tower.

The square opened before her, transfigured with snow, and empty. There was no mark of hoof or foot or wheel in the white thick-blanketed yard. Where had all the soldiers gone?

From a bare branch a single bird, a robin, looked down on her. Its throat was a songless tremor.

And now the swift-moving hands of the snow spun and wove about the princess a seamless vesture. Soon she was no longer a chaste statue in the barrack square. Her arms were sheathed in heavy flocculence. Her bosom was a white powerful curve.

The robin chirped from the bare tree, 'Follow me, I'll show you where your brother is. . . .' It flew away into the incessant wavering blizzard.

The princess yearned after the bird, but her feet had become rooted in a snowdrift. She threshed with her arms. She was suddenly free of the ground! She staggered in the air, she whirled, she was flying over barracks and guardhouse. Her new wings beat like a bell in the silence.

Below in the palace garden, the robin was perched in the heart of a rosebush. Its breast seemed like one of the scarlet blossoms.

Scalloped in snow, the roses were more beautiful than in the lucency of high summer.

The fountain beside the rosebush was frozen silent arches.

The princess glided down on the printless garden. The red-breast said in a bleak voice, 'This is your brother, this root, briar, rose. I'm sitting in his hair. One day in autumn the gardeners turned on him at last. Their pruning hooks and spades struck him, time after time. He died; they buried him. They hid him from the savage sun. I carried a seed in my beak and dropped it on his grave.'

The princess covered her face with her webs, and wept. 'Swans usually don't care about such unimportant things,' said the little shivering bird. 'Swans think proud beautiful deathless thoughts.'

The swan-princess uncovered her face. Indeed it was the beauty of her brother's change that had touched her heart, not the cruel edges that had been suddenly turned on him.

What was the matter with the palace? It stood there silent as a morgue. No winter music drifted from the gallery of the great hall. Where were the court ladies in their muffs and furs, moving perilously and soundlessly through the drifts? The lake did not ring with the noise of iron on ice. From the basement kitchens came no chef's curse and little scullery-maids' tremulous tearful answer, nor any enchanting tangle of cooking smells to thaw, later, the winter out of cold high-bred bones.

The swan-princess looked, and she saw that here and there the roof of the palace showed only naked rafters.

And the wrought-iron gate through which the poor folk from the slums of the city had shaken thin white fists that last summer – that was festooned with tattered rose-petals of rust. . . .

The robin chirped, 'The revolution wiped it all out. They've all gone into stories. You and I, we're changing too.'

'I see,' said the princess. 'I'd like to see my father and mother now, if you please, before I'm closed up in a book.'

The small bird leapt out of the rosebush and disappeared into high mazes of snow.

With a slow heavy clap of wings the swan-princess followed.

The great bell-beat, hung high, at last rose above the snow cloud, and the sun dazzled her with burst after burst of winter brightness. Far below, the little bird was a quivering dot, lost from time to time in fringes of snow-cloud. The swan surged on effortlessly. Splendours showered from her pulsing wings, a slow folding and unfolding.

Once the vast snow-cloud that seemed to cover creation split silently open. Through the chasm the princess could see a tract of the land her father had ruled – a hunting forest, a river. But something was wrong. Great gaps had been torn in the forest, and the scars were more than could have been wrought by axe or fire. The wide river, once so bustling and populous with trade, went on towards the sea heavy and black as treacle.

'This is the last winter of time,' said the swan-princess.

The cloud chasm closed up again, and she was left with the sun and, far below, the hesitations and spurts of the questing robin.

The smell of the sea was suddenly stronger than the fragile incense of snow. The robin dipped, dropped, disappeared. The swan-princess stooped.

Plunging down through the dark heart of the snow-cloud, she heard the ocean. She stooped again, perilously. She flew across flung veils of spindrift. A rising wave washed her feet.

There, on a stone of the beach, hung the robin, quite exhausted after its endless arches of flight across the last winter. The swan-princess dropped down on the sea margin. The heart of the little bird seemed to be quivering in its throat.

At last it cried, 'Look, swan, now, quickly! Here comes your father.'

A slow wave rose, hung, glittered, fell wounded on the wide beach, ended its reign in a hundred wondering whispers.

'The queen now,' panted the little bird. 'Look, look!'

A smaller wave stooped, curtsied, sang, spread itself in torn white fringes over pebbles and sand.

The two waves mingled their seethings and sighings, sweet unending sea voices, and withdrew.

'Life,' said the robin, 'doesn't last very long, does it? It's a very brief story.'

The swan-princess rose, hovered, tried to follow the two torn waves. But all those innumerable strands and drops were mingled inextricably with the ocean; for other intertwinings, other deaths and renewings.

The snow fell thicker. Time passed. The little bird was quilted in white. Its voice became a frozen crystal.

'Once upon a winter . . .' The swan-princess sang at the shore the lost legend. A silver key turned in her throat. Silent, unmoving, she was gathered into the pure crystal of time.

AN EPIPHANY TALE

There was once a small boy and he was deaf and dumb and blind.

He knew nothing about Christmas. All he knew was that it got cold at a certain time of the year. He would touch a stone with his fingers. His fingers burned with frost!

One day the boy was sitting on his mother's doorstep wrapped in a thick coat and scarf against the cold.

A stranger came and stood above him. There was a good smell from the stranger's hands and beard. It was different from the smell of the village people; the fishermen and the shepherds and their women and children and animals. The man smelt of sunrise.

The stranger touched the boy's ear. At once he could hear all the village sounds – the sea on the stones, his mother at the hearth baking scones, the seagulls, and the children playing in the field.

'No,' his mother was saying to the stranger, 'I don't want to buy a pan or a fork from your pack. No use speaking to the boy – he's deaf as a stone. Look, I'll give you a scone to eat. We're poor. I have no money to buy a thing.'

The boy didn't understand what the stranger and his mother said. The interchange of sounds seemed to him to be more wonderful than anything he could ever have imagined, and the most wonderful was the stranger's voice.

It said, 'Thank you for the bread, woman.'

Soon the stranger was no longer there. He had taken his rich silk smell and his clanging treasure away. The boy sat on the doorstep as the multitudinous harp of the world was stroked

again and again. His mother kneaded dough on the board and
stoked the peat fire.

Then the doors of his ears were closed once more. He laughed,
silently.

Another smell drifted across the boy's nostrils, different from
anything he had known. It was like incense of darkness, a
circling of bright swift animals.

The second stranger touched the boy's eyes. They opened.
The things he saw all at once amazed him with their beauty and
variety. A few flakes of snow were falling on the dead ditch-
grass. Gray clouds huddled along the sky. A cat crossed the road
from a fishing-boat below with a small fish in its mouth.

Two people were arguing in the door. The white strenuous
kind face must be his mother's. The black smiling face belonged
to the stranger. Both were beautiful.

The boy's looked into the gloom of the house. The flames in
the hearth were so beautiful it gave him a catch in the breath.

Clearly his mother was refusing to have anything to do with
the objects the stranger was spreading out before her: soft
shining fabrics, ivory combs, a few sheets with music and poems
on them. The boy did not know what they were – each was
marvellous and delightful in its different way.

At last his mother, exasperated, took a fish that had been
smoking in the chimney. She gave it to the black man. He smiled.
He tied up his pack. He turned to the boy and raised his hand
in a gesture of farewell.

The boy's mother shook her head: as if to say, 'There's no
point in making signs to this poor child of mine. He's been as
blind as a worm from the day he was born.'

Then, to her amazement, the boy raised a blue wintry hand,
and smiled and nodded farewell to the second stranger.

For an hour the boy's eyes gazed deep into the slowly-turning sapphire of the day. His mother moving between fire and board; the three fishermen handing a basket of fish from the stern of their boat to half-a-dozen shore-fast women; the gulls wheeling above; the thickening drift of flakes across the village chimneys; a boy and a girl throwing snowballs at each other – all were dances more beautiful than he could have imagined.

Then the luminous stone dulled and flawed. Between one bread dance and another, while his mother stood and wiped her flame-flushed brow at the window, she became a shadow. The boy was as sightless as he had ever been. He laughed, silently.

It was the most wonderful day the boy had ever known. And still the day wasn't over.

He was aware of a third presence at the door, lingering. This stranger brought with him smells of green ice, flashing stars, seal-pelts.

The mother, at her wits' end now, mixed with those smells of the pole her own smells of flour and butter and peat-smoke. The boy knew that his mother was angry; the smells came from her in fierce thrusting swirls.

It was enough to drive the most importunate pedlar away, but the man from the far north stood mildly at the threshold. The boy could imagine a bland quiet smile.

His mother's anger never lasted long. Another smell came to the boy's quivering nostrils: ale. His mother had poured a bottle of ale for the stranger, to refresh him for his journey. And now the smells of ice and fire and malt mingled gently in the doorway.

'I wonder,' thought the boy, 'what they're saying to each other? The same beautiful things as before, I expect. Their hands and their mouths will be making the same good shapes.'

It seemed a marvel to him that his ears and his eyes had been opened both in one day. How could any human being endure such ravishment of the senses, every hour of every day for many winters and summers?

The winter sun was down. The boy felt the first shadow on the back of his hand.

It was the time now for all the villagers to go indoors for the night. But this day they didn't go straight home. The fishermen and their wives and children came and lingered on the road outside the boy's door. He could smell the sweet milk breath of the children, and the sea breath of the men and the well-and-peat breath of the women. (Also he could smell the ashen breath of one old villager who would, he knew, be dead before the new grass.)

The villagers had come to stare at the stranger. The aroma of malt ebbed slowly. The boy felt the stone shivering; the stranger, having drunk, had put down his pewter mug on the doorstep.

Then he felt the touch of a finger on his locked mouth. He opened it. All his wonder and joy and gratitude for this one festival day gathered to his lips and broke out in a cry.

His mother dropped her baking bowl on the floor, in her astonishment. The bowl broke in a hundred pieces.

The old man who was soon to die said he had heard many rare sounds in his life, but nothing so sweet and pure as the boy's one cry.

The youngest villager was a child in her mother's arms that day. She remembered that sound all her life. Nothing that she heard ever afterwards, a lover's coaxing words, or a lark over a cornfield, or the star of birth that broke from the mouth of her own first child, no utterance seemed to be half as enchanting as the single incomprehensible word of the dumb boy.

Some of the stupider villagers said he had made no sound at all. How could he? – he had never spoken before, he would never utter a word again. A mouse had squeaked in the thatch, perhaps.

The stranger left in the last of the light. He joined two other darkling figures on the ridge.

The villagers dispersed to their houses.

The boy went indoors to the seat beside the fire. How flustered his mother was! What a day she had had! Her baking interrupted by three going-around men – her best blue china bowl in smithereens – her poor boy stricken with wonderment in the shifting net of flame shadows! She had never seen him like this before. He touched his ears, his eyes, his mouth, as if his body was an instrument that he must prepare for some great music.

And yet, poor creature, he was as dumb and deaf and blind as he had ever been.

The boy sat and let the flame-shadows play on him.

The mother washed her floury hands in the basin. Then she crossed the flagstone floor and bent over him and kissed him.

He sat, his stone head laved with hearth flames.

THE CHAMBER OF POETRY

The saffron-faced slant-eyed guest wrote his name in the book and said, 'Tell me, in what phase is the moon?' The innkeeper said, 'It's full moon two nights on.' The man smiled. He was shown up to his room. He ordered a crate of wine to be sent up, also three glasses. He said to the innkeeper, 'I shall not be requiring food.'

A girl went into his room to clean it next morning. He turned a smiling face on her, bright as the moon itself, and said he didn't mind dust, spiders' webs, or dead mice. The girl reported to the innkeeper that the Chinaman was writing at the table – the floor was littered with bits of paper, with pictures and brush-strokes on them; some pages torn in fragments. The innkeeper was curious about this guest. Occasionally he would listen at the keyhole: once he heard chuckles, and the tinkling of glass. A day and a night passed. On the third morning the chamber-maid went into the room. The man was not there. Papers with mysterious marks on them were strewn about the floor like a snow-drift. Also two of the glasses had been broken. The twelfth bottle of sack was dry.

There was an old gangrel body who carried gossip and curses and herbal remedies here and there about the land. She came to the inn door that same morning. The innkeeper threatened her with stick and dog. 'I just came,' she said, 'to tell you the queerest thing. That guest who never ate a bite or slept a wink, I saw him last night late. Wasn't he going back and fore on the riverbank, saying sweet and good things to the moon's reflection? Then he would hold out his arms to it for a while and be silent. Then once more he would declare himself to it like a man in love. I thought of going up to the poor crazy lad and asking, wouldn't I, a woman of flesh and blood, do instead of the moon's ghost? (Once I was a fine-looking girl.) But I had no time to do or say or think anything more, for the man gave a cry and leapt into the river and took the moon in his arms. Of course the moon broke into a thousand silver pieces. And when it was one and whole and round and trembling again, there was devil a sign of the crazy fellow. I just thought I would like to tell you.'

The innkeeper gave the old one a shilling for her information.

Then he looked into the guest-book and read the signature of his vanished guest: LI PO

That same inn, a day or two later, had another guest, a young country-bred lad who was hardly ever inside, fair weather or foul. He would set out early in the morning, sometimes before the sun was up, taking a few sandwiches with him, and a flask of milk, and an apple. When he came back, late, he seemed like a man who had seen things too marvellous to be spoken of. (But the innkeeper knew there were no marvels in that vicinity, only hills and forests and flocks, the village and the river.) Once the young man came back exhausted from a storm of wind and rain. 'I've blowed up your fire,' said the innkeeper. 'You can dry your clothes. I'll send the girl up with brandy and sugar and hot water. That'll put a glow on you!' But the guest told him, indignantly, that he wanted no such thing. Brandy, indeed! Stagnant water from the bog was purer and better than that burning trash! He had – he told the landlord – drunk it once, when he was a student. Never, never again! With a look of disgust he turned and went up to his room.

'That's a very strange young fellow,' said the landlord. 'That room seems to do something to a man.' (The brandy-hater was in the same room as the moon-lover.) And he said to the chamber-maid, 'Does he ever try to kiss you?'

'I'm a respectable girl,' said the chamber-maid. 'Just let him try.'

Along, of course, came the gangrel: to be threatened, as always, with shot-gun or the dog's tooth. 'Ah,' cried the old dark mouth, 'you're a kind man at heart – you wouldn't do such a thing. I want to speak about that young fellow you have staying in your inn. The queerest fellow I ever saw. I came on him yesterday, in the morning, beside the river. There he was lying his length, looking at a daisy, and I swear to God his eyes were brimming. And he's always around our tents, asking the old men and the young children questions – and as courteous as if we wandering folk were dukes and princesses. He writes down the nonsense we say in his book. I don't think it'll be long till that fellow is shut away for good. Watch him.'

The innkeeper gave the old one a mug of ale, and bought a dozen clothes-pegs from her.

Two days later Mr Wordsworth – that was the name of the guest – went away. He settled his bill; he was always strictly honest; and he told the landlord he was going to France, where at last (said he, his eyes shining), and for the first time, nature and man had lately been woven into a perfect accord.

In the public bar of the inn, every night, a group of young country lads – ploughmen, shepherds, rat-catchers – gathered for ale and coarse singing. By closing time they were all ruddy in the cheek. Some looked ready for a fight; others winked and nodded and said they had a meeting with this girl or that, in hedge or quarry. It was a boisterous crowd that moved away into the darkness. Then the innkeeper would lock the door, return to his counter, snicker, count the night's takings, and light the bed-candle.

One night the innkeeper discovered a country lad – the

melancholy one, Terence* – still lingering in the shadow.
Terence came once a week or so to the inn. He always kept himself a bit apart from the beer-swillers and the lechers; he seemed
to be more interested in the book he always had with him than
in the beer or the rough talk.

On this particular evening a ploughboy had poured the lees
of his ale over Terence's book, and a circle of merriment had
quickly gathered about the insulted one. Instead of offering to
fight, instead of storming out into the twilight, Terence had
gone meekly into the darkest nook of the bar; and there he had
continued to read sodden pages, and make a note or two, or
count out à rhythm on his fingers – occasionally pausing to look
across at the drinkers at the tables; and the landlord noticed how
envious and how compassionate those glances had been.

'Now, lad,' said the innkeeper on this particular night,
'spoiled your book, have they? They're rough ones, right
enough. You should cheer up, lad – get yourself a girl, eh? No?
Well, look here – I know you're a clever one, with your Latin
and your poetry – I have a vacant room upstairs. You can read
and write up there, and have your pot of ale sent up. Nobody to
disturb you there. All you'll hear is the singing of them and the
boasting of them and the clanking and the slurping of their cans
on a Friday night. What about that, eh?'

Terence thanked the innkeeper and said he'd like that – say
once a week, on a Friday night, when the silver and the ale-mugs
rang loudest along the counter. Every Friday night that summer
without fail he came to the vacant room in the inn, with his book
of Latin poems and his notebook and pencil.

'I bring him up his ale,' said the chamber-maid, offended,
'and he never so much as looks at me!'

And the gangrel wife said, 'That fellow, Terence, gives me
the creeps. Last night the old man and me were on the road,

* Terence was the name Housman used for the poet in *A Shropshire Lad*.

under the moon, going with the pony to the fair in the next village. There he was, in the middle of the road, pointing at an oak-tree. Says he, "A score of fellows were hanged there in times past, for thieving and wounding and saying dangerous things against the government. . . ." My old man gave the pony a wallop to hurry him on, and no wonder – wasn't his own great-grandfather a dangler from that very crossroads oak in his time!'

It drew on for autumn, and Terence stopped coming to the inn. He had taken his deep book-learning elsewhere, where it would be of more profit. The landlord found in the basket under the table, before winter, a hundred and more crumpled sheets of paper with bits of writing on them, poems. They all seemed to be about the drinking ploughboys and shepherds, and how they were all doomed, and were conscious of the shadow on their lives, and (but for a fleeting flower of happiness now and then) would never see ripeness and age. Gunshot, consumption, hangman's rope, would usher them out of time before they were thirty years old. . . . The landlord thought of the ruddy merry Friday-night faces, the lads for the girls and the lads for the liquor, and he laughed. Then he emptied the sheets of paper into the grate and put a lighted match to them.

The innkeeper called that room of his inn The Chamber of Poetry.

Once, the autumn before his death, he opened his guest book and looked at all the names of the people who, for shorter or longer time, had stayed in that room. His eye went from name to name: Li Po, Theocritus, Ovid, O. Khayyam, Sedulus Scottus, François Villon, Robt. Burns, John Keats, P. Verlaine, Ernest Dowson, A. E. Housman, G. K. Chesterton, Hugh MacDiarmid, Dylan Thomas. . . .

There was a dusty bottle on the shelf. A pewter pot hung at the wall. On the floor lay a broken quill.

A CANDLE FOR MILK AND GRASS

The *Saturnalia* was safe. After weeks of violent eastern storms, she was safe in the harbour of Hong Kong.

My father was Lloyd's agent in the island. No sooner was the telegram in his hand than he told me to go to a certain croft on the other shore of the island. I was to tell Hubert and Annie, of Troweart, that their grandson was safe.

I reached Troweart in the last light of a winter afternoon. I knocked. Two voices bade me enter.

Old Hubert was over by the window, reading and smoking his clay pipe. There was a scattering of books and magazines in the window seat. Annie was busy between the table and the open hearth. She was baking little yellow flat cakes on a griddle. She was white with meal to the elbows.

'Magnus is safe,' I said, when I got my breath back. 'Word's just come. The ship reached Hong Kong yesterday.'

'Well, well,' she said mildly, as if I had remarked that the fire was burning bonny in the twilight. 'Well, well.'

The old man continued to read and smoke.

The little yellow cakes, fretted round the edge, gave out a sweet fragrant smell. This was the only day of the year that such cakes were made.

I sat down on a stool near the door.

'We were born too soon,' said Hubert. 'We've seen steam, and the electric telegraph, and balloons. But that's nothing to the wonders that are coming. Nothing.'

'Is that so?' I said politely. 'I'll have to be going. My mother's

expecting me. It'll be tea time soon. I just came to say Magnus
is well.'

'Wait a bit,' said the old man. 'Listen to this, boy. You might
see it. But I won't. Nor will she.'

He bent his face upon the book. His spectacles flashed once
in the firelight. He began to read in a slow grave voice.

*The time is coming, is indeed not far off, when machines and
energies as yet unknown and untapped will do all the work of men.
Lamps will be lit without oil, a soft rich effulgence at the touch of a
finger. Nor will men have to go out with ploughs and harrows and
scythes, among dust and dung, in order to be nourished; nor will
they be required to take the knife brutishly to beast and bird and
fish. Our children will be nourished with balanced harmonious
chemicals, each according to the chemical needs of his body, and
none shall starve or be in want. . . .*

The little sun-cakes were ready over the peat-fire. Old Annie
set them, one after the other, on the clean hearth. She intoned:
'One for the table, one for the cupboard, one for a traveller, one
for birds, one for the poor cold bairn.' She stood looking down
at the yellow cakes with her hands clasped.

'You came between me and my book,' said Hubert. 'Do you
want to be ignorant to your dying day? You have no regard for
education. Keep quiet when I'm reading.'

I saw a gleam of bottles in the gathering darkness. In the far
corner a little wooden bucket was seething quietly. Annie took
first the ale bucket and then the chiming bottles over beside the
fire. Carefully she began to decant the ale, with a jug, from
bucket into bottles.

How the old man could see to read in all that cluster of
shadows I do not know. His eyes were used to horizons and
sheep-counts on a far hill. He resumed:

*The time is coming, children will be made in the laboratories of
science; they will be rational balanced healthy creatures. There
is no reason why the three score years and ten of our mortality*

should not be multiplied four-fold, or five-fold; yea, even more. . . .

The last dark bottle was filled and corked. Old Annie set them, one by one, against the wall. They twinkled merrily in the leaping firelight. She whispered: 'One for the fireside, one for the cupboard, one for a sad man, one for a songless man, one for the poor cold bairn.'

It was the second interruption. The old man closed his book with a clap and got to his feet. 'Annie,' he said, offended, 'I was trying to read something of importance to this boy, our visitor. I was trying to give him a vision of the day after his day. And all you do is utter that old superstitious nonsense! I'm going out. . . .'

He did go out, into the first stars and the night-song of the sea in the west.

I got to my feet soon after that. 'Mistress Hay,' I said, 'I have to be going home, now. I just came to say, Magnus is safe.'

'A good Yule to you, boy,' said Annie.

I had to stand outside and let the darkness wash my eyes for a time before I could find my way past the dwelling house. Next to it stood the byre. The byre door was open. A soft light wavered against the low flag-stone ceiling and the sharn-spattered walls. Inside, old Hubert was standing beside his one cow. In his hand he held an ox skull with a candle burning in it. The cow looked at him in wonderment.

'A good Yule to you,' said Hubert to the beast. 'Death and bread and breath. Give us butter and milk for a summer or two yet, will you?'

THE BOX OF FISH

They had had a good catch of haddocks in the afternoon.

Now it was evening. In the tarred shed above the shore the four fishermen were sitting round the cold bogey stove. The oldest one kneaded the blue back of his hand with urgent knuckles.

They had not gone home after mooring the *Sea Quest* and landing the boxes of fish. Instead they had sent the boy up to the hotel for a bottle of rum on tick.

They could see the whirls of snow through the window of the shed.

'We just got in in time,' said Alex. He dropped a lighted match upon the driftwood and coal and paraffin in the bogey. It roared into flame at once.

'We'll just have one dram,' said The Partan. 'Then home for tea. The wife'll be wondering.'

The boy came in out of the darkness, empty-handed.

'Mr Blanding said, "No cash, no rum",' said the boy. '"Tell them that," said Mr Blanding. "There's more than ten pounds against The Partan on the slate," he said.'

They spent more than five minutes discussing the hotelier's character in the blackest of terms.

'You see them boxes of fish,' said Tim Smith to the boy. 'Tell him, a box of haddocks for a half-bottle rum.'

The boy took the box of fish in both hands and staggered out with it into the darkness.

A quarter of an hour later he was back with a half-bottle of rum.

'There's cups in the cupboard,' said a man with a black beard, Dave the skipper.

The boy brought over cups, darkly stained with ancient tea, and gave one each to the four fishermen round the bogey stove.

'What did you see in the village?' said The Partan to the boy. 'Did you see Mary-Ann looking for me?'

'No, I didn't,' said the boy.

Dave the skipper gravely dropped four musical measures of rum into the cups, one after the other. Rich Caribbean fragrances mingled with the smells of salt and tar.

'I saw two strangers,' said the boy. 'They were looking for a place for the night. They didn't look to me as if they could afford the hotel.'

Alex smacked his lips. 'There's worse things,' he said, 'than a drop of rum on a winter night.'

Tim set down his empty cup on the floor.

'Go and tell Mary-Ann,' said The Partan to the boy, 'I'll be home in ten minutes. Tell her we had a good catch.'

The boy went out into the night. It had stopped snowing. The sky had cleared. In at the open door stars throbbed cold and brilliant.

The boy was back in five minutes. Mary-Ann had told him to inform James (The Partan) that she didn't care when he came home, if ever. His tea was spoiled anyway. She would rather have the house to herself than have a poor thing of a drunk man snoring in the armchair beside the fire. She was in no hurry to see him. She had this Yule cake to bake. He would just be in the way.

The empty half-bottle lay on the floor.

The skipper laughed. 'Well,' he said, 'there's no hurry in that case. We deserve a drink. We've had a cold hard day of it.'

Three heads nodded about the ruddy stove.

The boy said he had glimpsed the two strangers between the

store and the kirk. They still didn't seem to have found a place.

'Boy,' said the skipper. 'You see that box of fish against the wall. Take it up to the hotel. Mr Blanding will give you a half-bottle of rum for it. Hurry now.'

The top half of the bogey was red-hot. At the dark window snowflakes whirled and drifted, a horde of gray moths.

Alex licked the last drop of rum from his moustache.

At the end of half an hour the boy had still not returned.

'What can be keeping him?' said The Partan.

'Maybe Blanding wouldn't deal with him,' said Tim. 'Maybe Blanding thinks he's got enough fish for one night.'

They waited another ten minutes. Nobody spoke.

'What I'm feared of,' said Dave, 'is that he might have gone over the pier in the blizzard.'

They waited till the thick-falling snow had dwindled to a few gray loiterers under the star-flung sky; then they put on their bonnets and oilskins and blew out the lamp. It was all right – there were still five boxes of fish at the wall. They went, one after the other, up the stone steps to the village street.

At the hotel Mr Blanding said no, he hadn't seen the boy since the rum-fish transaction earlier in the evening.

The four fishermen went and stood at the edge of the pier, looking down. It was ebb-tide. They saw no broken body on the stones surrounded by a silver scattering of fish.

They trooped to the boy's house. The mother opened the door to them. 'You don't need to worry,' she said. 'Sam's done exactly what you told him to do. Old Ezra's had his fish, and blind Annie, and that cripple boy at the end of the village. Who else? Sam's been at a dozen poor doors – the ones you told him to go to. At the end of it he had two fish left. He told me about the hippies or beatniks or whatever you call them – he's out now looking for them.'

'That's all right,' said the skipper. 'We were just wondering.'

Sam's mother invited them in for a drop of something, seeing it was Yule time. But they said they'd better be getting home. There was another blizzard building up in the north.

POETS

THE SATIRIST

Tung Wo, the master poet, one summer day wrote a poem about the mountain and the men and women and children who lived there. The villagers and the shepherds came to Tung Wo's house to hear the poem. They clapped their hands enthusiastically at the end. Some of the listeners had been mentioned in the poem. One covered his face with his hands. Tung Wo bowed and went indoors to his fire and his wine-bottle.

The villagers, sated with poetry, walked home along the road. It was the night of the new moon. As they went they discussed, with much laughter, the poem. The man in charge of the vineyard said, 'It is very true what Tung Wo said in the poem about you others, but it isn't true what he said about me, that I put water in the wine I make. How does he know that? I resent it.'

They walked on in silence for a while. A child straggling and running at the back of the company, said, 'My grandfather has to drink twice as much wine now before he is merry.'

The villagers went on, reciting bits of the poem and smiling.

The blacksmith said, 'What was that Tung Wo said about me – that my iron is brittle and rusts at the first drop of rain? He is not such a good poet as he is said to be. Let me tell you, the lord from beyond the river sent to me ten years ago to make a gate for his garden.'

The villagers walked on. The little boy whirled about and chanted, 'The horses of this mountain have broken hooves.'

The keeper of the village gate said, 'I have a good mind to bring Tung Wo before the court. What a scoundrel, to say I visit the girl Sing Va when I ought to be guarding the gate. You

all laughed and clapped at that part of the poem. Has the tiger come into the village at night? Have the robbers troubled you, them from the caves higher up, the murderers? Tung Wo will be made to answer.'

The villagers walked on in silence. Sing Va, conscious of veiled looks all around her, began to cry. The boy took her hand and walked along beside her.

They were half way home.

The man who had been nominated village chief for that year said, 'Did I hear right? I think I must have nodded off and dreamed at a certain part of Tung Wo's poem. It seemed that Tung Wo accused me, in the most entertaining and melodious way, of keeping some of the tax money I gather on your behalf for the lord beyond the river. If Tung Wo actually said that, the lord will have to be told. The lord will send for his lawman, maybe the executioner.'

The villagers, walking down the slope, murmured like angry bees.

Who listens to the nonsense of a child? The child stumbled on a stone. The child picked himself up. The child said, 'Why has a double lock been put on the oak chest in the treasury where the tax roll is kept?'

The lady who was in charge of the silk looms said, 'It is a waste of silver to keep a poet in idleness on this mountain, especially a poet who says I keep the best silk for myself and only wear it at night, when all the village lamps are out, to entertain lovers. The man is a liar and a danger to our community. Besides, he is impotent.'

The other women moved away from the maker of silk. The child cried to a bird in the first tree, 'Tung Wo has lain in a dark dream between the blouse and the trousers.'

'Ah well,' said the philosopher as the first houses of the village came into sight, 'doubtless poetry is an evil thing and a corruption in any community. The art is all the more sinister in that the beauty of it makes a catch in the breath. The kingdom would be better without lutes and pipes. I did *not* get my wisdom from So Van in his porch beyond the two rivers.'

The feet of the villagers slurred in the dust. It is a long walk from the house of the poet to the village gate.

Only the child danced along. 'A nightingale for a silver cage,' he sang, 'not an old parrot.'

The rich village merchant had said nothing on the road. His face had begun to smoulder in the poet's garden. Tung Wo had referred in the course of his satire to a certain dealer in fleeces and wood and gold who, in the market-place of the city, dealt crookedly and shamelessly with the produce of a certain village; one who manipulated and twisted numbers; who bought and sold girls for money; who kept a rotten ship on the river, so that the previous winter seven sailors had been drowned; who because of the evil that he did made the name of that village stink throughout the entire region and beyond. . . .

The merchant spoke to no one on the road. He kept his eyes on the dust.

By this time the villagers had passed through the village gate. They separated in the square. The innocent ones, except the child, went through this door and that. Lamps were lit.

In the square lingered the vintner, the smith, the guardian, the chief of that year, the silk weaver, the philosopher, the merchant. They moved about each other. The merchant snapped his fingers violently. Silent, they looked into his russet face. The merchant jerked his head, vehemently, towards a certain house far back along the road by which they had come.

The child began to weep.

When the same moon was full, one night the poet Tung Wo was set upon in his garden by masked men. They struck him, they stabbed him, they upset his wine jar, they tore his hair.

A girl came as usual to light the poet's fire next morning. She found him lying as if he had been mauled by a tiger.

The villagers said it must have been the bandits from the cave higher up who had killed Tung Wo. They wrapped him in a green coat and laid him in the earth, and planted a tree above him.

The lord beyond the river sent another poet to the village. That one's poetry was all about birds and lions, demons and ghosts.

The child grew up. As soon as the first hair was on his lip, the lord beyond the river had him enrolled in the college of poetry and music a thousand miles down-river.

Ten years later a company of travelling players arrived in the village. It was the first company to visit the village for a long time; the village had an evil reputation throughout the region of the two rivers. They performed their masque in the village square. The masks worn were the stylized masks of the Grape Treader, The Worker in Metals, The Keeper of the Folk, He who Speaks for All, The Spreader of Heavenly Cloths, The Finder of Hidden Wisdom, The Honest One.

Beautifully they moved about one another. Gravely and well they spoke. The earth seemed the richer for being trodden by those inspired dancers. It seemed indeed for an hour as if the gods had sent messengers down among men.

They praised wine making, and the intricacies of working in silver and iron. They praised the principle of subtlety-with-strength, and the idea of the community as pyramid and as cloud, and the beautiful treaty signed between worm and tailor. They praised the highest wisdom which is more quiet and beautiful than a glass of water. They praised all forms of trade and barter, whereby distant cities bow one to the other across immensities of desert or sea.

The villagers, when the seven maskers finally turned their backs, were too enchanted to strike their hands together, even. At last the spell was broken, the village square fluttered with smiles as though a hundred butterflies had come on the wind.

Five of the seats were empty however. The occupants of those seats had risen up during the performance and stolen away. Then the audience heard weeping from another seat. The lady of the silk looms, who was too old for love now, cried as if her heart was breaking.

'Where is the other?' said the bamboo cutter. 'Where is the one who used to buy and sell for us? The lord beyond the river sent for him a year ago. He has never come back. I have heard that he and the lord's executioner had a rendezvous one morning. I wish that man had been here.'

The leader of the players turned round. He stepped forward. 'You have heard these words before,' he said. 'Satire and hymn are two sides of the same gold piece.'

Then the villagers threw blossoms on to the stage. Under one of the masks was a known face. A young man opened a jar of wine on the steps of the fountain.

Even the old weeping lady smiled after a time, as though perhaps there might be a possibility of forgiveness for her also.

THE SKALD IN THE CAVE

Arvid was the earl's skald; he was reckoned to be one of the finest poets in the north.

Arvid's father had been the earl's skald before him, and also his grandfather. The same ivory harp was used by the three poets.

Now Arvid began to count his gray hairs. He was tired at last of rune and kenning and alliteration. He began to wither about his harp.

'Your skill is leaving you, Arvid,' said the earl. 'What am I to do for a new skald?'

'One of my sons will follow me, of course,' said Arvid.

Arvid had five sons. At least three of them were ambitious to become the earl's skald. Their father had patiently taught them the craft, winter by winter, in their youth. They were passable wordsmiths, no more. It was possible that one of the three might suddenly utter oracular language. But in general poets are at their best in their twenties, and the three harp-striking sons of Arvid were over the crest of the hill. The west was in their eyes, and the sunset.

'Which of your sons do you recommend?' said the earl. 'Thord?'

Thord Arvidson lived in the island of Sanday. He had a large farm there, and a beautiful wife, and three ships that traded between the Baltic ports and Orkney.

Thord was a busy man, and all the cares of the island lay on him. He judged fairly and dispassionately whenever a lawsuit was brought before him: lobster creels rifled, for example, or a haystack burnt. His judgements were thought to be a fine blend of strictness and charity.

To restore himself after a hard day's work Thord Arvidson would recite poetry in his hall – sometimes his own, sometimes old poetry from Iceland or Norway. He was listened to with respect and pleasure. Sometimes a drunk man would raise his ale-horn and roar out, 'Well made, poet.'

'Not Thord,' said Arvid.

'You are perhaps thinking of Ottar,' said the earl.

Ottar Arvidson was a famous man on the northern way, and southward and westward too. He worked his father's farm in Birsay, but the truth was that he didn't much care for that kind of life. When the oxen were yoked in spring, and the plough began to turn the earth over, there came a glitter in Ottar's eye. 'The ship!' he would shout to the shepherds and the falconers. 'Get the *Valiant* out of the shed. See that she's caulked. See that the women put a better barrel of ale on board than last year's gut-rot. The boy who looks after the geese – he's grown tall and thick-shouldered this past year. Put him down for an oars-man. . . .' Ottar could hardly wait to get the seed locked in the earth. He was more in the boatshed than in the barn, all the month of March.

At last the day came. The *Valiant* was launched. The crew climbed aboard. Here and there a girl wept among the looms. A graybeard raged because he was reckoned to be too old this year for the spring cruise: he would rather fall on the shore of Grimsby or Dublin than wheeze out his life among the milk-and-corn-smelling women. The sail quivered at the mast. The oars struck the water, raggedly at first, then (to the chant of the helms-man) with a fluent powerful rhythm.

Ottar Arvidson was off on another viking cruise.

Always hitherto he had returned, laden with booty: linen from Ulster, silver from the churches of the west, dark-haired girls from this or that 'glen of weeping'. Ottar was reckoned to be a lucky viking. It was a privilege to sail with such a fortunate and daring man. Sometimes when they got home there was a gap here and there on the rowing-benches, but that was to be ex-pected. Once Ragna got her man home – he had only one arm though he had set out with two. 'What kind of cloth will you weave from now on?' Ragna had said to the weaver. 'All you can do now is feed the cat.' But the one-armed weaver got a larger share of loot than the others that year.

They came back always when the corn was changing from green to gold.

After harvest, Ottar would begin to work on his poem, in which he set out with style and gusto the whole story of the voyage: heroism, rapine, death. So the winter nights on the farm were made splendid and resonant by the voice of Ottar Arvidson, farmer, viking, and poet. What though occasionally he exaggerated the taking and burning of a village in the west? What though he said of the weeping women: 'The viragos would have scratched our faces off, but Harald drove them back with a broad blade. . . .'? The story was much improved thereby. The whimper of the goose-boy at the ford at Maldon became a shout of victory. The ploughmen and the shepherds – that their womenfolk thought ordinary enough creatures – became heroes in Ottar's verse.

'Not Ottar,' said Arvid.

'I will send for Rolf as soon as he gets back from his latest philanderings,' said the earl. 'The ivory harp will be his.'

Rolf Arvidson and his women and his night visitings were famous from Iceland to Caithness.

He was the earl's tax-man. His duty was to visit every farm in the earldom and assess it for purposes of taxation. In consequence Rolf was not the most popular man in the north. The farmers did not vie with each other to set him down in an honoured place at their boards. Many lies were told to Rolf, in the way of figures, numbers, estimates; but Rolf had the knack of entering the true amount in his ledger.

The only ones who smiled when Rolf came about the farms were the women.

He was not made welcome at the boards, but the door of the chamber of the women stood always unlatched when it was known that Rolf the tax-man was coming. He entered it always at night. There he was given the best food from the kitchen, and the ale that had honey in it. There he was given sweet red mouths. There, after the candle was blown out, he was given everything.

The early fishermen, going down to the beach, would see before dawn a furtive shadow detaching itself from the solid shadow of the farm – from that part of it where the women slept.

The strange thing was that the man was ugly, with a thick brutish mouth and eyes that squinted a little.

Attempts were made, from time to time, on the life of Rolf Arvidson. A farmer made poor by the heavy demands of the tax-man would wait for him at the end of a dark road. The fathers and brothers and sweethearts of beautiful soiled girls would carefully plan an 'accidental' death for Rolf. He would be discovered some fine morning under a crag, broken; or drowned in a quarry. ('Your lordship, I take leave to break to you a sad piece of news. Your faithful steward and factor, Rolf Arvidson, was found dead this morning, early, among the rocks under the Red Head. This is a great grief to us all. Convey our sorrow to his aged father, the skald. Rolf must have gone over the cliff in the darkness. He did a great deal of his business by night. . . .')

But that elegiac epistle was never sent. Rolf never took the road of death. He seemed to have some inner knowledge whenever a mischief was plotted against him. Always on these occasions he spurred on his horse by another road. . . .

Rolf said once to a poor farmer, Gunnar Stye in the island of Hoy, 'Gunnar, congratulations. You have a fine farm here. You've cultivated it well. The earl will be pleased when I tell him. Fine barley, good oats, the greenest grass I ever saw. Cattle, sheep, pigs in excellent condition. Your tax is as follows – a hundredweight of butter, a hundredweight of cheese, and a hundredweight of malt. See that they're ready for me to uplift the first day of November.'

'Would you ruin me?' cried Gunnar. 'I can't pay that much! Would you make me and my daughter beggars on the road?'

'That is the assessment,' said Rolf.

At that moment Gunnar's daughter came in from the byre

with a bucket of milk. She set it down in a corner. She smiled at Rolf and went out again.

'Gunnar,' said Rolf, 'that's a handsome girl you have.'

'We have been on this farm since the time of my great-great-grandfather,' said Gunnar. 'It was he, new from Norway, who first broke this glebe. Since that day we have been loyal men to the Earl of Orkney. He had only to raise his hand and we would come to his bidding, we and all our men. We fought for him and we toiled for him. We were the earl's men, always. Now this is our reward – the earl, through his tax-man, will ruin us.'

'She is as pretty a girl as I have ever seen,' said Rolf. 'What's her name, Gunnar?'

'Brunna and I – what'll become of us? I will have to sell the farm for what I can get for it. Brunna will see that I don't stave. Brunna is a good girl.'

'Brunna is very beautiful,' said Rolf. 'Now I must go to the farms in Rackwick. I will be back in the morning to confirm the assessment.'

Rolf spoke to Brunna at the end of the oatfield. Gunnar saw them, standing in his door. Then Rolf mounted his horse and rode off between the hills.

An early fisherman, going down to his boat, saw before sunrise next morning a furtive shadow detaching itself from the solid shadow of the farm of Braewick. It was not the shadow of Gunnar (he was gross as a pig: hence his nickname).

About noon the next day Rolf Arvidson returned to Braewick farm.

'Go away,' said Gunnar. 'You have ruined me. Have you come to crow over a ruined man?'

'Gunnar,' said Rolf, 'I have been thinking about the tax assessment. It seems to me now that I overestimated somewhat the fertility of your farm here. When I looked at some of the other farms, I saw that yours was rather poor in comparison. Consequently I am going to reduce the assessment.'

'I'm pleased to hear that,' said Gunnar.

'Brunna – I don't see her this morning,' said Rolf. 'Commend me to her. Well, the assessment. It seems to me, Gunnar, that you have been over-taxed for some years past – in fact, ever since the earl appointed me to be his tax-gatherer.'

'I never thought I was under-taxed, indeed,' said Gunnar.

'I have been coming here,' said Rolf, 'since Brunna was a little girl. She has grown to be very beautiful and very talented. Gunnar, in view of the fact that you have been overtaxed for seven years, this year you will be exempted from taxation.'

'Thank you,' said Gunnar. 'Thank you, Rolf, very much.'

'I will see how things are when I come back to Hoy next year,' said Rolf. 'Brunna must be a great help to you on the farm.'

'She is,' said Gunnar. 'She works hard, the girl. Only, Rolf – this is a strange thing – she's still asleep. It's past noon! The cows are needing to be milked. Just listen to them mooing at the byre door. I don't understand it. Brunna has never slept so long before – never. . . .'

As to the poetic abilities of Rolf Arvidson, it is difficult to discuss them, for nobody had ever heard the man recite verses, his own or those of others, for twenty years.

It is known that his father instructed him in verse-craft in his youth, and said he was an apt pupil. Thereafter Rolf, if he practised his art at all, did it in secret. I suppose there are poets who compose and recite for themselves alone; if so, their art is maimed and fruitless.

It is more likely that Rolf turned the energy that could have made him a good poet into that other channel: that peters out at last in bogs and marshlands.

Rolf had no children in the islands that are known of.

'Certainly not Rolf,' said Arvid.

*

'Now, Arvid,' said the earl, 'you have only two sons left. Solmund won't do. He's in Eynhallow. I can't pluck him out of the monastery to be my skald. The abbot wouldn't like that. Besides, Solmund might not want to come. Besides, again, I don't think he ever learned verse-craft.'

'Psalms and bits of scripture,' said Arvid. 'That's all the singing Solmund does. They don't call him Solmund in that place. They call him Brother Helvetius. You never heard such a monotony as drifts out of that chapel, eight times a day. Dark voices, bright voices, a midnight mingling, a noontide weave. The same few psalms and bits of gospel, over and over, as if that was the music of eternity, the seamless garment, and the poems made on farm and shipboard are, in comparison, patches sewn together, a scarecrow's coat. No, Solmund will not be exchanging his bridal garment for our rags and tatters.'

'In that case,' said the earl, 'I will have to look elsewhere for a skald. I am sorry about that. I had hoped to keep the office in your family, Arvid.'

'I have another son,' said Arvid. 'His name is Jon.'

How came you, in all this House of Man, to this one forbidden door?

A dark and devious way, instructed by ghosts, listeners, knowe-dwellers.

Who gave you the key?

It is my own forging. I turned from the instruction that the master skald gave to the easy ones and the glib ones. I forged my own key in silence and in secrecy. Listen. I have brought a poem to this threshold.

You have found the door. Will you be invited to enter?

Those inside will judge, once my mouth has opened a few times in the ritual way. Listen.

Answer this. What is the mystery of a name? What is any word but certain stoppings of the breath, a clownish conjunction of tongue and lips and teeth and palate?

None. Nothing.

Inside, there is only this: celebrations of name and word.

Not as they are spoken in the merchant's booth, or squandered as the women do spreading out clothes beside the burn. Wind passes, grass and stone are silent again. A secret language, whereby for example there are other words for the word 'fish', and for the word 'corn', and for the word 'heart', and for the words 'man and woman', and for the word 'sleep', and for the word 'death', and for the word 'grave', and for the words 'body' and 'ghost', and for the word 'kingdom'. Those essences of language known to the poet alone have great beauty, so that men with ordinary speech are moved often to tears or to joy. All hungerers, whether for food or love or light, find in these arcane orderings of sound a bread that can sometimes satisfy them. A coward puts on a coat of courage against the dragons: age, death, darkness. Young he dies, though he has seen a hundred winters. Without our oracles and orisons is neither dignity nor delight for the brutishness of blood and bone. But listen.

How have you prepared yourself for this craft?

By a way of negation. I was not in the fighting ships, among the blood and the gold. Women allured and tormented me – I let my flesh ebb from them. I have not raised my voice in any debate. When Arvid drew diagrams for my brothers in the sand, I studied rather the drifts of cloud and sea. I was not among those who cried out with penitence under the arch. I learned only to put a stitch in a net. I can bind sheaves in a harvest. That much I intruded into the affairs of men.

What do you expect to find in this room?

Ghosts. Skulls. Shadows of what is to happen and what has happened. A loom. A lamp. I have this urgent poem to speak here in the doorway, now.

We are listening, man. Enter. Begin.

*

When it had heard, the guild of skalds opened the curtain to Jon Arvidson. The curtain dropped again. No man can say what ceremony was enacted inside the cave; perhaps a robe or a ring was put on the youngest son, and taken away again, and locked in a chest for the next poet, whenever he might come, perhaps next year, perhaps a century later. Others say that no such ceremony ever took place, and there is no such thing as a guild of poets.

Later that day, in the presence of the earl, Arvid gave the ivory harp out of his withering hands into the open hands of Jon.

LORD OF SILENCE

Kirsty MacBeth was heavy with her fourth child. One winter night when Colm was at a meeting of the men there came a knock on her door. Kirsty was nervous, on account of her condition. At first she was unwilling to draw the bar. Who knows what thief or fool or outlaw might be abroad in the darkness? Kirsty looked at her children asleep on the straw. The wind howled in the chimney. At last Kirsty went and opened the door.

An old gangrel woman stood out there in the wind and the rain. 'Mistress,' she said to Kirsty, 'I'm cold. Can I eat a crust of bread at your fire?'

In the end it was more than a crust she got to eat at the fire that Kirsty blew into red flames. She got broth and a bit of fish and oatcakes and cheese and a sup of whisky. She mumbled blessings between every mouthful. At last she had had enough. She licked her withered fingers.

'Blessings on all this household,' she said. 'What are they, sleeping in the corner?'

'My three daughters,' said Kirsty.

'And where is the man of the house?'

'He's on the mountain.'

Then the old one began to say black things about men. Men

were selfish cruel creatures, one and all. A tall cruel drover had
broken her heart fifty years ago. Since that dreadful day she had
been on the roads, a beggar – she that once had been the most
beautiful girl in the glens. . . . Such was the baleful power that
men had over women. On the mountain, were they – in that cave
on the mountain, planning the next cattle raid, so that there
would be plenty of beef and cheese next summer? Nothing of
the kind. She had seen them all drinking at sunset in the
shepherd's hut, with chorus and boast and challenge in plenty.
That was the way it was with men. They were liars, one and all.
Blessings on the four good women of this household. . . .'

'My Colm is a good man,' said Kirsty, 'and kind to our
children.'

'He has put another burden upon you, I see,' said the old
woman. 'They don't care what women have to suffer. Oh no.
When the delight is over, it's out of the door with them before
daylight. The long slow agony they leave for us women to
endure. Let them drink then in the shepherd's hut.'

'I'm glad that I'm soon going to be the mother of Colm's son,'
said Kirsty.

'Well now,' said the old woman, 'it's me for the road again. In
the wind and the mists. I must go till the end of time.'

But Kirsty made a bed of straw for her in the corner.

Before she dropped off to sleep among her daughters, Kirsty
heard the old woman muttering to herself, 'How does the kind
one know that it's a man she'll bring into the world soon? She's
right. I will not put a blessing on any boy or man, the carriers of
sword and seed. But for the man-child that will be cradled in
this kind house, I ask from the elements the gift of poetry.'

When Kirsty woke early in the morning the old woman had
gone.

Colm came home at noon, blear-eyed and sheepish. The
cattle-raid, it seemed, would not take place after all. The pass
was too well guarded. Seeing that the plotters had come so far,

and some of them hadn't seen each other for a year and more, they had passed the night in the shepherd's hut, with a dram or two, and a song, and stories.

Kirsty kissed the gaunt gray cheek.

When the child was only a few days old they realized that something was wrong with him. He had uttered no sound at the time of his birth. Now it seemed he would utter no sound for ever.

Kirsty prised open the perfect little mouth. There was nothing wrong with the red curl of tongue or the small sweet warm cavern of the palate. . . .

'This was to have been a bard,' said Kirsty to Colm. Then she told him about the visit of the old gangrel woman, and how, on the verge of sleep, she had overheard the grudging prophecy about the unborn child.

As the years passed, Duncan grew in silence among his laughing singing boisterous sisters. Silently he laughed, silently he grieved (the tears streaming down his face). Delight over-brimmed from eyes and mouth at sound of the wind, at sight of the scarlet and black tatters of sunset, at the leap of the deer-hound on the mountain. What moved him most – what made him shake his head in wonderment – were the stories men told of the true king across the sea, and how the Scotsmen of the sheep-hills and ship-ports had sworn allegiance to a fat uncouth German upstart. . . . All things good and bad the boy gathered within a circle of silence.

He grew up. He was a young man. He learned to hunt, to herd, to plough. He learned to drink from the silver cup, pledging his companions in silence. His father went once on a cattle raid into the next glen, and did not return. They managed to get his body from the scree before the eagle and the wolf made their narrowing circles. The women of the glen, who mourned in a ritualistic way, had never seen such stark grief on a human face: the mouth of Duncan opened in a black silent wail.

The sisters married, one after the other. Kirsty and her tongue-locked son lived together at last.

He fell in love, the young man. To everyone there is a time for loving. When his hour struck, Duncan did not choose any of the women and girls who had put always a circle of kindness and care about him. He chose (love is the deepest of mysteries) the one flaw in that circle. It was on a sly lazy lewd creature that he bestowed all his hoard of affection. He could not have enough of Shona's company, outdoors or indoors. He was always bringing gifts to her – a plate of venison, a cairngorm, a silver coin.

He led her over his mother's threshold once as if she was a princess. Mother and sweetheart had no liking for each other. The meeting of Kirsty and Shona that day was like two swords clashing.

The girl seemed to take pleasure in putting barbs and stings into her silent lover. A herdsman would come on Shona half way along the mountain, coming down like a goat, laughing, sometimes looking back. Further up, and there Duncan stood behind a rock with tormented eyes and trembling fists; he would return no greeting to the herdsman as he went past.

One winter evening all the glen folk saw and heard how Shona used her man. She was all smiles to him at the ceilidh, when the voice of the story-teller had fallen silent and the whisky was going round. Her unwashed cheek dimpled at him, she stroked the clustering gold ringlets of his hair and beard. How he glowed and melted to the touch of her! Pair by pair the young men and women sought that night a dark corner; some stole quietly out to the starlight. When at last, with pointings to the door and hand-urgings, Duncan beseeched his lady that they should do likewise, all of a sudden she was a snow woman. She was hurt and offended. She was a good girl, she let him know in a voice loud enough for all to hear, and growing louder. She wasn't like some of the other shameless sluts. She knew what was right and what was wrong. She had learned commandments and catechism. Let him leave her alone, the dumb fool that he was! . . . Then the insulted one gathered her shawl about her and went over and spent the rest of the night among the married women and the widows.

To see Duncan's brimming eyes then, his clenched fists, his trembling mouth – nothing could have been more pathetic or moving! He went home, alone, long before the ceilidh was over.

Yet there he was, the very next morning, at the slut's door, with a token of reconciliation: a looking-glass he had bought from a pedlar. She had the hurt look still on her face as she took it from him. At last she gave him a wintry smile. The boy was as grateful for that as if she had dowered him with gold and silks and a herd of cattle.

So this love affair went on all one winter and spring. Then, one day, the girl was suddenly out of the glen, she was up and away, she departed without a farewell or a godspeed.

At the end of the third day Duncan knocked at the door where Shona's mother lived. His eyes were loaded with pain.

'Is it Shona you're wanting to know about? She's been at the fishing bothies lately, at night, whenever boats are in from the west. Lazy useless slut! That Oban skipper came to shelter in the loch at the weekend. What are you looking like that for, boy? Have you seen a ghost? Fish-guts, that's all she's good for. I tell you this, you're well rid of her, though she's my own daughter. I don't care though I never set eyes on her again. . . .'

Then, once more, Shona's mother turned to the kneaded clothes and the gray broken water in her tub.

Next day Duncan was out of the glen too. He vanished, silent as a thaw.

*

Word came to the glen of a new bard who had arrived suddenly, nobody knew from where, among the mountains. It was Fergus the wandering man who brought the news, together with bits of politics and scandal. That was the year before the first royal war against the Hanoverian; there was much unrest in that part of the stolen kingdom.

This was a great bard, Fergus declared, who had come among the Gaels. His poems were pure and passionate. The dust of the old men was stirred by his love songs. His poetry of war and valour caused the young men to look longingly at old claymores and daggers. He had only to utter a word like 'rose'; then the young women would begin to weep or to laugh with delight.

Had Fergus seen and heard this bard? the folk wanted to know.

No, said Fergus, he had always arrived at a clachan just after the bard had gone away again, or else just before the bard was expected (one who begs his food, like Fergus, cannot wait too long in one place, especially – as then – when there was great poverty everywhere).

'And what is the name of this famous singer?' asked the weaver. (The news Fergus brought was always taken with a pinch of salt.)

Fergus did not know. There were many mysterious things about the bard. He seemed to have no true name; or rather, in this village or in that castle or in the other glen various names were given him: such as, 'bee-mouth', or 'drinker at the well of love', or 'bard with the yellow circles about the face', or 'the awakener of steel'. But, said Fergus, in truth these names were poor attempts in poetical jargon to describe the enchantment he spread everywhere. He was anonymous. If he had a name it was a hidden name.

There were other mysteries about the bard. Most poets are only too pleased to have the patronage of this lord and that chief; they sleep on softer beds than groomsmen and smiths; they drink from silver quaichs at the high table. Not this bard. He slept and ate with the poorest people. It was like a royal feast, the breaking of those crusts in a ditch. He signed the food always with a gray silent devout cross.

Nor did anyone know his birthplace or parentage.

'And when,' said Neil of the Stags, 'may we expect to have the honour of entertaining this great bard in our poor glen?'

Again, Fergus did not know. The bard went like the wind where he wanted to go.

The mysterious singer never visited the glen. That year, later, certain of the clans marched against the red-coat army of the Hanoverian, and poetry was forgotten in the shouts of war and clashing of steel. Twelve young men left the glen to fight for the true king. Nine of them came home again, some with wounds. With them they brought home Duncan MacBeth. He had been in the battle also. Duncan had fought well, they said. 'There are two red-coats who will not kiss or curse again because of Duncan. . . .' Duncan had been wounded on the mouth by a bayonet – there was a long silver transverse scar – it lay like a key across his lips. It seemed to be a last pledge of silence.

The great bard was killed, some said, in the battle. Young men described his ruined face after the cannonade had fallen silent, and his broken harp, and the fouling of golden hair with blood and smoke.

Others said no. The bard had moved south and then west into Ireland, where poetry was a more honourable estate than in this usurped land.

Others said again that the bard had never existed. Hope, delight, danger had quickened the west at that time. Through such swirling mists men and women imagine marvellous harp-strokes.

*

Till the day of his death, many years on, Duncan was a silent man. He looked after his few cattle. He had a contented dram or two on a winter's night in the shepherd's hut. His mother died one autumn. Duncan folded her hands dutifully.

He lived to be an ancient man, all silver and parchment. Some said he was more than a hundred when he died. He never looked at a woman again with either longing or lust.

When at last he went silent into the great silence, the young priest was brought over from the island. The priest, standing at the open grave, spoke his fine Latin commending Duncan into the keeping of angels and saints. The dumb man was now, it seemed, part of the one everlasting hymn of praise around the throne of eternity. Then the priest scattered a handful of clay over the body.

It is said that when the priest had closed his prayer-book, but before the gravedigger began to shovel in earth and stones, a beautiful woman in a grey shawl came down the mountain path. She passed through the group of mourners and looked into the grave. 'Farewell,' she said, 'great poet of this glen, my dear one, lord of silence.'

Then the stranger turned again and disappeared into the mists.

GOLD DUST

'Is the post past?' said Bridie Kern to Mrs Scully. The garden-fence was between them. Mrs Scully was hanging up towels to dry. Streams of bright wind went over the council house gardens.

Mrs Scully removed two pegs from her teeth and said, 'I don't know.'

'Frankie's expecting a letter,' said Bridie Kern; as if the meagre intelligence was a spell or an intimation of immortality.

*

'The weed's expecting a letter,' said Mrs Scully to Mr Paton. 'What kind of letter would ever come to the likes of him?'

The garden-fence was between them.

Mr Paton was turning over his potato patch.

'His social security,' he said.

'His social security comes on a Friday,' said Mrs Scully. 'He's always up for *that*. He meets the postman half-way down the street.'

Mr Paton smiled and shook his head. He stuck his glittering spade in the earth.

Bridie Kern said in Somerville's, 'Ten tins of beer. It's for a party. A few of Frank's friends. Make it a dozen cans.'

'Frank's birthday?' said the licensed grocer.

'No, it isn't. It's a more important day than his birthday. It's never happened before. There'll be one or two red faces along Chapel Street when the word comes. Did you see the post?'

'Two pounds exactly,' said Mr Somerville.

'He's got himself a bird,' said Ida Innes the newsagent and tobacconist. 'He picked up some girl at the dance on Saturday. I saw them. There they were, standing in the door of the Free-masons'. I have to go up that close, you know, to get home. It was Frankie all right. I don't know who the bird was. Some lass from a farm, I think.'

'God help her,' said Mrs Scully, 'if she thinks that creature 'll ever do anything for her.'

'He'll be expecting a love letter,' said Ida. '*The Daily News*, is it?'

'Love letter!' said Mrs Scully. 'Love letter! Do you think that trull of a mother of his would be treading the pavement like the

Princess Royal all morning for that? Her paragon – sharing her paragon with another female.'

'You would have thought their mouths were stuck together,' said Ida Innes.

'I hear,' said Guthrie the scavenger, 'there's been money won on the pools along this street.'

'Is that so?' said the new young policeman.

'I know the fella to see,' said Guthrie. 'Doesn't have a job. Fred or Frank or some name. A right layabout. That's his mother, her with the bag of beer crossing the street.'

'If you win a big sum on the pools,' said Police-constable Stevenson, 'a telegram comes. Then a man flies up in a private plane from Liverpool.'

'It's just what I heard. Good luck to him,' said Guthrie.

'The post's taking a terrible time today,' said Bridie Kern to the tree in the presbytery garden. 'I wonder is he past? Frankie'll be that hurt if it doesn't come today. There'll be some red faces. None of them have had boys that were delicate from the time they were born. Frank'll be remembered when them and all their trash of sons and daughters are dust. They'll say, "Frank Kern was born in Chapel Street, in that house over there," in the years to come. . . .'

A blackbird in the priest's tree made response to Bridie Kern's pride with a burst of immaculate lyricism.

'I wonder,' said Bridie, 'should I knock on Father Mac-donald's door and tell him? He'll be that pleased. I just know what he'll say. "Well, now, Bridie, I always knew the boy had something in him. A Robbie Burns for Alandale – well, well, well. And when will we be reading the poem? God bless you, now, Bridie. . . ." He's sure to say something like that. I would

knock at the door, too, but there's that housekeeper of his taking
cold looks at me from the edge of the curtain.'

'The worst thing that ever happened to the youth of this
country,' said Mr Somerville to the man who was cleaning the
street and the man who was preserving the queen's peace along
Chapel Street and environs, 'the very worst thing, in my
opinion, was when they abolished conscription. There's that
poor woman, Bridie. She's out of her house every morning from
before seven till after ten cleaning banks and offices, to keep that
thing in idleness. A dozen cans of export, if you please. Some
great word that's coming with the post. So poor Bridie can't go
to her work this morning. (That's three pounds she's losing.)
She must wait for this letter. The best letter that could ever be
delivered to that young man would be from the Army, like in the
old days, calling him up. They'd knock some sense into him
there! They'd soon let him see what was what! There she is, the
poor soul, peeping round the corner of Paterson's Close, seeing
can she see the postman. And her owing more than five pounds
from the weekend. Lord Muck must have his cigarettes and his
Coca-Cola.'

'Good luck to him,' said Guthrie.

Eck Quoyle the postman turned out of Main Street at 10.41 a.m.
precisely. He called at seven doors along Chapel Street, includ-
ing a door marked *Miss Bridget Kern*. He dropped a large thick
envelope through the letter-box. Then he walked briskly down
the garden path and turned right at the corner and disappeared
down Bank Street.

Francis Kern, a quarter of an hour or thereby later, carried the

same large thick envelope (ravaged now at the flap) out through
the front door of number 9 Chapel Street.

He walked slowly across the street towards 'The Lion of
Scotland' bar.

His progress was observed from certain windows along both
sides of the street: by Bridie Kern his mother, by Mrs Scully
(widow), by Mr Thomas Paton (retired postal sorting clerk), by
Mr Somerville the licensed grocer, by Mrs Ida Innes the newsagent and tobacconist, and by the priest's new nameless housekeeper from Uist.

Police-constable Stevenson had been summoned elsewhere
by tinny noises on his 'walkie-talkie'.

Guthrie was turning into Aberavon Street when he saw from
the corner of his eye the young man and the mysterious envelope.
He began to sweep the pavement of Chapel Street for the second
time in one morning, back towards the door of 'The Lion of
Scotland' – a thing never known before.

It was five minutes after opening time that Frank Kern entered
the bar. He was the first customer.

Frank asked for a pint of heavy.

While George the barman was drawing the beer Frank withdrew from the envelope what appeared to be a book or a catalogue. The title, in large crude smudgy type, was DIGGINGS
– *A New Verse Quarterly*.

'What's this then?' said the barman. ('Twenty-five p.')

Frank, after consulting the page of contents, opened the
magazine at another page. The paper had the texture of oatmeal.
With his free hand Frank dredged coins out of his hip pocket
and set them on the counter.

Mr Paton entered the bar: a thing never known before. (Mr
Paton drank moderately, and in private, at home or in his
friends' houses.)

Frank indicated to George an inch of cyclostyled type with his thumb. 'Something I've had published,' he said. 'A poem.'

The barman studied the page. Frank observed George over a thinning ellipse of foam. Mr Paton approached the counter, smiling.

At the doorway of 'The Lion of Scotland', neither out nor in, lingered Mrs Scully: a thing not known before. Mrs Scully was a great temperance woman.

George whistled. 'Is this you then, Frank? Did you write this?'

The poet nodded, gravely.

'Well done, Frank,' said George. 'I didn't know you went in for this sort of thing. Poetry, eh. Good luck anyway, pal.'

Guthrie's brush rasped the doorstep of 'The Lion of Scotland'. It drove Mrs Scully willy-nilly in across the threshold.

Mr Paton expressed interest. He asked if he might read the poem. He had always been interested in literature, he said. The magazine, open at the correct page, was passed across. Mr Paton studied Frank's poem for some time, his lips moving. At last he said it was good, in his opinion. Modern, of course, and difficult. No rhyme. You needed to read that kind of poetry a few times.

Frank lit a cigarette and drew the smoke deep into his lungs. He coughed twice into his clenched fist. Then he said, 'I'm busy on another poem. The editor wants more.'

'Can I get you something, madam?' called George the barman to Mrs Scully. Mrs Scully shook her head and looked confused: a thing hardly known before.

'I'll have a small vodka and orange,' said Mr Paton. 'Feel the need, after digging that garden. Your mother will be proud of you, Frank. Give Frank whatever he wants to drink, George.'

The scavenger had gone back to his trolley.

Bridie Kern could be seen on the opposite pavement, lingering and looking. (Like Mrs Scully she had never darkened the door of a public house in her life; nor would she, even on such a proud day.)

Mrs Scully was heard to whisper, 'He must have copied it out of some book.'

A pint of heavy beer, Mr Paton's tribute to literature, was set down in front of the poet.

The priest's housekeeper, a shopping basket in the crook of her arm, had stopped near Bridie on the street. They exchanged words (a thing not known till now). Bridie nodded her head, and smiled. The housekeeper gave one swift look into the dark interior of 'The Lion of Scotland', and passed on. Bridie lingered still, looking through the open door at the shadowy figures inside.

Mr Paton took a sip from his small glass of vodka and orange. He adjusted his spectacles. Once more he bent earnest brows upon the grey paper. He nodded once or twice.

Mrs Scully withdrew.

George asked Frank if there was much money in poetry. Frank looked grave. He raised his pint. He sent proud plumes of smoke down his nostrils.

Six coal miners came in and made for the counter, talking about horses and bets.

The curve of the poet's upper lip was richly crudded with foam.

Frank accepted the magazine from Mr Paton. He put it back quickly in its envelope, to be safe from the black hands of the miners.

KING AND SHEPHERD

The armies of the desert king poured on. A city at the bend of a river was surrounded, besieged, starved into submission in a week. (The common people would have endured much longer – it was the merchants and senators who decided to negotiate, and they after all had the say in that town.) It so happened that negotiations on the part of the desert king were simple and swift: the decapitation of the leading merchants and senators, once the gates were open.

Torches were thrust into wooden houses on a day of high wind. The city burned for a week.

Somehow or other the common folk survived by salvaging odds and ends, snatching brands from the fire, and patching up shelters for themselves. In the midst of their appalling suffering and privation they experienced bits of luxury: they unearthed flagons of wine from rich cellars, and smoked sturgeon and silk coats. (The desert king's men had overlooked those things, or else set no value on them.)

The horsemen of the desert king poured west.

They came to the shore of a great inland sea. They gazed, astonished, at the grey ruffled water that stretched to the horizon. Hitherto the only waters in their experience had been rivers, lakes, wells, marshes, fountains and rain-drops. 'This is the great sea,' said the desert king, 'that surrounds the rich earth like the white of an egg. Of this sea I am also king.' He cut a wave with his sword. And indeed all the incoming waters seemed to bow down at his feet, an innumerable conquered host.

The hordes from the desert, sweeping along the margin of the

sea, arrived at another city and surrounded it and prepared for a
siege. They were surprised that no arrows, stones, insults or
chamberpots were emptied over them. That night the silence of
the city kept the king awake. At first light he looked out from his
tent. The gate of the city stood open. The soldiers fed their
horses, then breakfasted on locusts and flat thin bread and the
sharp beer of their country. There would be no battle, they were
told. They formed into rough ranks behind the king and the
chiefs (it was not in any true sense a disciplined army). Then
they all poured in through the gate and along the streets to the
square with its palace and its great church. Everywhere there
was silence and emptiness. Their slant eyes looked uneasily
around them. Houses and booths and churches were bare. Ten
thousand people had vanished.

At night the desert king gave his men the consolation of a
stupendous fire. The wooden city burned – the sky glowed and
the inland sea mirrored the red and black shifting magnificence
– millions of stars rose out of the conflagration to meet the
steadfast stars.

That was another night without sleep for the desert king.

Next day, as they were preparing for a new westward surge, a
horseman approached the king and said, 'I think I should be
getting home. I would like to be there in time for the lambs. The
women know little or nothing about lambing.' (I said these men
had no discipline and no notion of heroism and the hand of
destiny; nor, if it comes to that, of the clash of dynasties brought
about by the marvellous workings of history and trade, decay
and renascence. . . .) The ignorant yokel was awarded a thousand
lashes for wasting the king's time.

Spectacular things – like dismemberments, impalings, de-
capitations, the burning of cities – that was what delighted the
tent-dwellers and hillmen of the east. That was why they followed their king, who had once been a poor man like themselves;
those amazing carnivals of destruction, as well of course as the

loot and girls picked up along the irresistible way – and the sheer joy of storming into the dangerous unknown.

It seemed that all the people of that vast region had melted before the advance of the desert king.

They raged through silent coastal towns and villages. The herds too had been driven into the hills. For a month, as spring came on, the conquerors lived on insects and roots and wild birds. 'Sea!' shouted the desert king on the shore one day – 'I am your lord. Deliver me a tribute of fish – the silver flashing ones and the ones with the hard blue armour on them, also a million of the little twisting ones that live in small sea houses.'

The ambassadors of the sea, the breaking waves, seemed to kneel to the king and promise all. But in the end the sea, conquered though it was, gave them nothing out of its vast treasuries, neither pearls nor fish nor salt.

It was now early lambing time.

The horsemen, horde after horde, leaned into the west: flying manes, curling whips, slant inscrutable eyes. They broke new horizons.

Towns and villages burned behind them. They ate snails. They ate the eggs of wild birds. Hundreds died from drinking out of wells that the inhabitants had poisoned.

One morning, after a meagre breakfast, the desert king ordered a count to be made of his army. It was reported to him that ten thousand soldiers had deserted in the past three weeks. They had stolen out of their tents by night. They had turned the heads of their horses and ridden home. There was one chief, a brave and a cheerful man, whose army was less by twelve hundred horsemen. The desert king had this man – a friend of his, and one of his truest counsellors – stood against a wall and shot to death with arrows.

'There is a city in the west,' said the desert king, 'called Rome.

There is a city called Corinth. There is a city called Vienna. There is a city called Paris. The cities we have conquered are poor things compared to the cities that have not yet seen us. The doors of those cities are made of gold. The women are whiter than swans. You will sleep in beds of silk beside girls whiter than swans. . . .'

The hordes turned their backs on the sea and streamed westward. Towns and hamlets burned behind them.

They saw only one living man in a thousand miles, an old shepherd. In normal circumstances he would have been swept up like a piece of driftwood in a torrent. On this morning the desert king halted beside the old man. The whole vast army – horses and men – came to a halt.

The old man had just delivered a ewe of two small fluttering lambs. He looked up at the conqueror and his huge host.

'So you're the people I was told about,' said the shepherd. 'The duke sent his man along all the villages in this valley last week. "Get out fast," said the duke's man. "The slant-eyed host is on the way, the yellow barbarians. Take all your cattle and sheep and swine and make for the hills. Take as much food and blankets as you can carry. Leave nothing for those murderers. Hurry now – hurry!" That's what the duke's man said. So they all packed and went away – all except me. "Come on, Sergei," said the village elder, "we're going now. . . ." "It's all right for you," says I, "but I have two ewes here, Mags and Curly, that are going to have difficult labour," I says, "and they're not fit to walk up among the mountains, and what'll become of them," says I, "if I leave them now? Besides," says I, "it's cold in them mountains at night, not good for my cough. And anyway," I says, "I'm too old to care what the savages do to me. Not that they'll ever notice me in the first place. They're after more important things than a shepherd and two sheep and three or four lambs."'

These were the exact words of the shepherd to the king, but

of course the king did not understand a single word. It was all strange mouth-music.

The horsemen who were near enough to see and hear wondered what their king would do with this old creature. There would only be enough mutton to make a dinner for the king and the chiefs. For the host it would be, again, wild eggs and roots, hedgehogs and mice and birds and frogs.

'Father,' said the king to the shepherd, 'you've got the lambs out of that ewe – well done – but you'll have a harder job with black-face there. It looks to me like a fatal blockage, that. I know what I'm talking about. When I was a lad I brought out hundreds of lambs. Of course. My father was a shepherd – we all had to work. I think that was the happiest time of the year, lambing, even though it was cold hard work and often in the darkness of night, with my brother holding a lighted torch. Yes, it was good – even though my father would flog us if we lost a lamb, and us not to blame. That ewe now – that delivery – I admit that would have been too much for me – for me or for my father or for you now, old one.'

The old man delivered the lamb safely, a red tatter, and set the spindly thing adrift on the hill. The ewe heaved to its feet and went after the lamb.

The desert chiefs had never heard their king speaking that way before – maybe one or two of them had who remembered him as a young man before a certain conjunction of stars lured him on to glory.

The shepherd smiled at the shepherd-king. He had not of course understood a single word of that barbaric utterance; but it was to him a music that mingled easily with his own homely words. Two men had meshed their voices into one song.

He turned back to his tiny flock.

The host thundered west for another five days. Charred wood and stone everywhere. Now the villagers were setting fire to their houses and barns before the barbarians arrived; so that even the consolation of flames was denied them.

One morning on the east bank of a great river the desert king, hungry, addressed his famished army. 'Men,' he cried, 'it's not we, you understand, who are going to conquer Rome and Vienna. I hope none of you thought that. I have made it clear from the beginning that we are more path-finders and explorers than conquerors. Our great task was to make a beginning, to find out the way. This we have done. It is enough for you and for your generation. The further west we go the more formidable the armour and the towers will be. If we venture too far we will be cut off and destroyed. We will not see our hills or our sheep again. We have smelt the rich winds of the west. Now we must go home. We must prepare a greater host than this. It will take a long time. I think it may be my grandson who will ride in triumph through the gates of Vienna!'

He gestured. Seventy-five thousand faces turned to the east. The chiefs gave scattered orders. The hooves made desolate thunder along the endless steppe by which they had come.

They rode in silence, except that one or two men in the rear ranks grumbled that the lambing would be over by the time they got home: and the lambing ale all drunk, most likely.

They passed the same shepherd in the same field with his five sheep. The shepherd-king saluted the shepherd. Thousands of shepherd-soldiers saluted the lonely shepherd. He gave them a flutter of his hand.

About a century later the great-grandson of the desert king led his hosts into the west. His name was Genghis Khan, and he rode further than his simple ancestor.

ANDRINA

Andrina comes to see me every afternoon in winter, just before it gets dark. She lights my lamp, sets the peat fire in a blaze, sees that there is enough water in my bucket that stands on the wall niche. If I have a cold (which isn't often, I'm a tough old seaman) she fusses a little, puts an extra peat or two on the fire, fills a stone hot-water bottle, puts an old thick jersey about my shoulders.

That good Andrina – as soon as she has gone, after her occasional ministrations to keep pleurisy or pneumonia away – I throw the jersey from my shoulders and mix myself a toddy, whisky and hot water and sugar. The hot water bottle in the bed will be cold long before I climb into it, round about midnight: having read my few chapters of Conrad.

Towards the end of February last year I did get a very bad cold, the worst for years. I woke up, shuddering, one morning, and crawled between fire and cupboard, gasping like a fish out of water, to get a breakfast ready. (Not that I had an appetite.) There was a stone lodged somewhere in my right lung, that blocked my breath.

I forced down a few tasteless mouthfuls, and drank hot ugly tea. There was nothing to do after that but get back to bed with my book. Reading was no pleasure either – my head was a block of pulsing wood.

'Well,' I thought, 'Andrina'll be here in five or six hours' time. She won't be able to do much for me. This cold, or flu, or whatever it is, will run its course. Still, it'll cheer me to see the girl.'

*

Andrina did not come that afternoon. I expected her with the first cluster of shadows: the slow lift of the latch, the low greeting, the 'tut-tut' of sweet disapproval at some of the things she saw as soon as the lamp was burning. . . . I was, though, in that strange fatalistic mood that sometimes accompanies a fever, when a man doesn't really care what happens. If the house was to go on fire, he might think, 'What's this, flames?' and try to save himself: but it wouldn't horrify or thrill him.

I accepted that afternoon, when the window was blackness at last with a first salting of stars, that for some reason or another Andrina couldn't come. I fell asleep again.

I woke up. A gray light at the window. My throat was dry – there was a fire in my face – my head was more throbbingly wooden than ever. I got up, my feet flashing with cold pain on the stone floor, drank a cup of water, and climbed back into bed. My teeth actually clacked and chattered in my head for five minutes or more – a thing I had only read about before.

I slept again, and woke up just as the winter sun was making brief stained glass of sea and sky. It was, again, Andrina's time. Today there were things she could do for me: get aspirin from the shop, surround my grayness with three or four very hot bottles, mix the strongest toddy in the world. A few words from her would be like a bell-buoy to a sailor lost in a hopeless fog. She did not come.

She did not come again on the third afternoon.

I woke, tremblingly, like a ghost in a hollow stone. It was black night. Wind soughed in the chimney. There was, from time to time, spatters of rain against the window. It was the longest night of my life. I experienced, over again, some of the dull and sordid events of my life; one certain episode was repeated again and again like an ancient gramophone record being put on time after time, and a rusty needle scuttling over worn wax. The shameful images broke and melted at last into sleep. Love had been killed but many ghosts had been awakened.

When I woke up I heard, for the first time in four days, the sound of a voice. It was Stanley the postman speaking to the dog of Bighouse. 'There now, isn't that loud big words to say so early? It's just a letter for Minnie, a drapery catalogue. There's a good boy, go and tell Minnie I have a love letter for her. . . . Is that you, Minnie? I thought old Ben here was going to tear me in pieces then. Yes, Minnie, a fine morning, it is that. . . .'

I have never liked that postman – a servile lickspittle to anyone he thinks is of consequence in the island – but that morning he came past my window like a messenger of light. He opened the door without knocking (I am a person of small consequence). He said, 'Letter from a long distance, skipper.' He put the letter on the chair nearest the door. I was shaping my mouth to say, 'I'm not very well. I wonder. . . .' If words did come out of my mouth, they must have been whispers, a ghost appeal. He looked at the dead fire and the closed window. He said, 'Phew! It's fuggy in here, skipper. You want to get some fresh air. . . .' Then he went, closing the door behind him. (He would not, as I had briefly hoped, be taking word to Andrina, or the doctor down in the village.)

I imagined, until I drowsed again, Captain Scott writing his few last words in the Antarctic tent.

In a day or two, of course, I was as right as rain; a tough old salt like me isn't killed off that easily.

But there was a sense of desolation on me. It was as if I had been betrayed – deliberately kicked when I was down. I came almost to the verge of self-pity. Why had my friend left me in my bad time?

Then good sense asserted itself. 'Torvald, you old fraud,' I said to myself. 'What claim have you got, anyway, on a winsome twenty-year-old? None at all. Look at it this way, man – you've had a whole winter of her kindness and consideration. She brought a lamp into your dark time: ever since the Harvest Home when (like a fool) you had too much whisky and she supported you home and rolled you unconscious into bed. . . . Well, for some reason or another Andrina hasn't been able to come these last few days. I'll find out, today, the reason.'

It was high time for me to get to the village. There was not a crust or scraping of butter or jam in the cupboard. The shop was also the Post Office – I had to draw two weeks' pension. I promised myself a pint or two in the pub, to wash the last of that sickness out of me.

It struck me, as I trudged those two miles, that I knew nothing about Andrina at all. I had never asked, and she had said nothing. What was her father? Had she sisters and brothers? Even the district of the island where she lived had never cropped up in our talks. It was sufficient that she came every evening, soon after sunset, and performed her quiet ministrations, and lingered awhile; and left a peace behind – a sense that everything in the house was pure, as if it had stood with open doors and windows at the heart of a clean summer wind.

Yet the girl had never done, all last winter, asking me questions about myself – all the good and bad and exciting things that had happened to me. Of course I told her this and that. Old men love to make their past vivid and significant, to stand in relation to a few trivial events in as fair and bold a light as possible. To add spice to those bits of autobiography, I let on to have been a reckless wild daring lad – a known and somewhat feared figure in many a port from Hong Kong to Durban to San Francisco. I presented to her a character somewhere between Captain Cook and Captain Hook.

And the girl loved those pieces of mingled fiction and fact;

turning the wick of my lamp down a little to make everything more mysterious, stirring the peats into new flowers of flame. . . .

One story I did not tell her completely. It is the episode in my life that hurts me whenever I think of it (which is rarely, for that time is locked up and the key dropped deep in the Atlantic: but it haunted me – as I hinted – during my recent illness).

On her last evening at my fireside I did, I know, let drop a hint or two to Andrina – a few half-ashamed half-boastful fragments. Suddenly, before I had finished – as if she could foresee and suffer the end – she had put a white look and a cold kiss on my cheek, and gone out at the door; as it turned out, for the last time.

Hurt or no, I will mention it here and now. You who look and listen are not Andrina – to you it will seem a tale of crude country manners: a mingling of innocence and heartlessness.

In the island, fifty years ago, a young man and a young woman came together. They had known each other all their lives up to then, of course – they had sat in the school room together – but on one particular day in early summer this boy from one croft and this girl from another distant croft looked at each other with new eyes.

After the midsummer dance in the barn of the big house, they walked together across the hill through the lingering enchantment of twilight – it is never dark then – and came to the rocks and the sand and sea just as the sun was rising. For an hour and more they lingered, tranced creatures indeed, beside those bright sighings and swirlings. Far in the north-east the springs of day were beginning to surge up.

It was a tale soaked in the light of a single brief summer. The boy and the girl lived, it seemed, on each other's heartbeats. Their parents' crofts were miles apart, but they contrived to meet, as if by accident, most days; at the crossroads, in the village shop, on the side of the hill. But really these places were too earthy and open – there were too many windows – their feet drew secretly night after night to the beach with its bird-cries, its cave, its changing waters. There no one disturbed their communings – the shy touches of hand and mouth – the words that were nonsense but that became in his mouth sometimes a sweet mysterious music – 'Sigrid'.

The boy – his future, once this idyll of a summer was ended, was to go to the university in Aberdeen and there study to be a man of security and position and some leisure – an estate his crofting ancestors had never known.

No such door was to open for Sigrid – she was bound to the few family acres – the digging of peat – the making of butter and cheese. But for a short time only. Her place would be beside the young man with whom she shared her breath and heart-beats, once he had gained his teacher's certificate. They walked day after day beside shining beckoning waters.

But one evening, at the cave, towards the end of that summer, when the corn was taking a first burnish, she had something urgent to tell him – a tremulous perilous secret thing. And at once the summertime spell was broken. He shook his head. He looked away. He looked at her again as if she were some slut who had insulted him. She put out her hand to him, her mouth trembling. He thrust her away. He turned. He ran up the beach and along the sand-track to the road above; and the ripening fields gathered him soon and hid him from her.

And the girl was left alone at the mouth of the cave, with the burden of a greater more desolate mystery on her.

The young man did not go to any seat of higher learning. That same day he was at the emigration agents in Hamnavoe, asking for an urgent immediate passage to Canada or Australia or South Africa – anywhere.

Thereafter the tale became complicated and more cruel and pathetic still. The girl followed him as best she could to his transatlantic refuge a month or so later; only to discover that the bird had flown. He had signed on a ship bound for furthest ports, as an ordinary seaman: so she was told, and she was more utterly lost than ever.

That rootlessness, for the next half century, was to be his life: making salt circles about the globe, with no secure footage anywhere. To be sure, he studied his navigation manuals, he rose at last to be a ship's officer, and more. The barren years became a burden to him. There is a time, when white hairs come, to turn one's back on long and practised skills and arts, that have long since lost their savours. This the sailor did, and he set his course homeward to his island; hoping that fifty winters might have scabbed over an old wound.

And so it was, or seemed to be. A few remembered him vaguely. The name of a certain vanished woman – who must be elderly, like himself, now – he never mentioned, nor did he ever hear it uttered. Her parents' croft was a ruin, a ruckle of stones on the side of the hill. He climbed up to it one day and looked at it coldly. No sweet ghost lingered at the end of the house, waiting for a twilight summons – 'Sigrid. . . .'

I got my pension cashed, and a basket full of provisions, in the village shop. Tina Stewart the postmistress knew everybody and everything; all the shifting subtle web of relationship in the island. I tried devious approaches with her. What was new or strange in the island? Had anyone been taken suddenly ill? Had anybody – a young woman, for example – had to leave the island suddenly, for whatever reason? The hawk eye of Miss Stewart regarded me long and hard. No, said she, she had never known the island quieter. Nobody had come or gone. 'Only yourself, Captain Torvald, has been bedridden, I hear. You better take good care of yourself, you all alone up there. There's still a grayness in your face. . . .' I said I was sorry to take her time up. Somebody had mentioned a name – Andrina – to me, in a

certain connection. It was a matter of no importance. Could Miss
Stewart, however, tell me which farm or croft this Andrina
came from?

Tina looked at me a long while, then shook her head. There
was nobody of that name – woman or girl or child – in the island;
and there never had been, to her certain knowledge.

I paid for my messages, with trembling fingers, and left.

I felt the need of a drink. At the bar counter stood Isaac Irving
the landlord. Two fishermen stood at the far end, next the fire,
drinking their pints and playing dominoes.

I said, after the third whisky, 'Look, Isaac, I suppose the
whole island knows that Andrina – that girl – has been coming
all winter up to my place, to do a bit of cleaning and washing and
cooking for me. She hasn't been for a week now and more. Do
you know if there's anything the matter with her?' (What I
dreaded to hear was that Andrina had suddenly fallen in love;
her little rockpools of charity and kindness drowned in that huge
incoming flood; and had cloistered herself against the time of
her wedding.)

Isaac looked at me as if I was out of my mind. 'A young
woman,' said he. 'A young woman up at your house? A home
help, is she? I didn't know you had a home help. How many
whiskies did you have before you came here, skipper, eh?' And
he winked at the two grinning fishermen over by the fire.

I drank down my fourth whisky and prepared to go.

'Sorry, skipper,' Isaac Irving called after me. 'I think you
must have imagined that girl, whatever her name is, when the
fever was on you. Sometimes that happens. The only women I
saw when I had the flu were hags and witches. You're lucky,
skipper – a honey like Andrina!'

I was utterly bewildered. Isaac Irving knows the island and
its people, if anything, even better than Tina Stewart. And he
is a kindly man, not given to making fools of the lost and the
delusion-ridden.

                              *

Going home, March airs were moving over the island. The sky, almost overnight, was taller and bluer. Daffodils trumpeted, silently, the entry of spring from ditches here and there. A young lamb danced, all four feet in the air at once.

I found, lying on the table, unopened, the letter that had been delivered three mornings ago. There was an Australian postmark. It had been posted in late October.

'I followed your young flight from Selskay half round the world, and at last stopped here in Tasmania, knowing that it was useless for me to go any farther. I have kept a silence too, because I had such regard for you that I did not want you to suffer as I had, in many ways, over the years. We are both old, maybe I am writing this in vain, for you might never have returned to Selskay; or you might be dust or salt. I think, if you are still alive and (it may be) lonely, that what I will write might gladden you, though the end of it is sadness, like so much of life. Of your child – our child – I do not say anything, because you did not wish to acknowledge her. But that child had, in her turn, a daughter, and I think I have seen such sweetness but rarely. I thank you that you, in a sense (though unwillingly), gave that light and goodness to my age. She would have been a lamp in your winter, too, for often I spoke to her about you and that long-gone summer we shared, which was, to me at least, such a wonder. I told her nothing of the end of that time, that you and some others thought to be shameful. I told her only things that came sweetly from my mouth. And she would say, often, 'I wish I knew that grandfather of mine. Gran, do you think he's lonely? I think he would be glad of somebody to make him a pot of tea and see to his fire. Some day I'm going to Scotland and I'm going to knock on his door, wherever he lives, and I'll do things for him. Did you love him very much, gran? He must be a good person, that old sailor, ever to have been loved by you. I *will* see him. I'll hear the old stories from his own mouth. Most of all, of course, the love story – for you, gran, tell me nothing about that. . . .' I am writing this letter, Bill, to tell you that this can never now be. Our granddaughter Andrina died last week, suddenly, in the first stirrings of spring. . . .'

Later, over the fire, I thought of the brightness and burgeoning and dew that visitant had brought across the threshold of my latest winter, night after night; and of how she had always come with the first shadows and the first star; but there, where she was dust, a new time was brightening earth and sea.

MAGI

THE FIRST MAGUS

They told him, suddenly one morning, that he was the king.

'No,' said Hwa Su, 'I am only the prince of the mountain kingdom.'

The First Secretary said, 'Sire, you are the king.' He knelt and kissed the boy's hand. One by one the palace officials knelt and kissed Hwa Su's fingers and whispered 'majesty'.

'My father is the king,' said Hwa Su. 'My father has gone down-river with the horsemen to see the Emperor. It was a summons. He will be home in two days.'

Hwa Su was alone soon in his chamber. He drifted on silken feet through rooms and terraces and corridors. He came on his tutor writing on a piece of silk. 'The palace officials,' said Hwa Su to the tutor, 'have been behaving strangely to me all morning. They call me "king". Are they taunting me? Is it a game?'

'How should I know?' said the tutor. 'Go away. I am busy writing down, before it is too late, the history of this small beautiful kingdom. Go away and play, boy.'

Hwa Su wandered all afternoon through the gardens and the pavilions. The palace was very quiet, and had been ever since the soldiers and the horsemen had gone with the king down-river to visit the Emperor.

In the pavilion of the musicians only one musician sat. The music that came from his flute was the most desolate music Hwa Su had ever heard. 'Play some butterfly music,' cried Hwa Su. The man with the flute made among the blossoms a black star of music.

Hwa Su walked beside the river. The fishermen working at

their nets suddenly folded their nets when they saw the boy coming and leapt into the boats and rowed out into the current. An old blind fisherman said, 'Hwa Su, lord, I smell you coming on the wind. I smell the silk and the gold. Hwa Su, better you had been born a poor boy, like my grandson. Hwa Su, the evil times are coming, and soon.'

'No,' said Hwa Su, 'for the harvest is good this year. Two new gold mines have been opened in the mountains. We have begun to exchange goods with the Tartars. My father the king says that soon this mountain people will be well off.'

'Beware,' said the blind man, 'when a little poor kingdom becomes suddenly a little rich kingdom. Then the kingdoms round about join hands. Then the Emperor begins to smell revolt and insurrection and independence.'

Hwa Su plucked a rose and put it in the blind man's hand.

Hwa Su wandered back through the garden. The pavilion of the musicians was empty. The bamboo flute lay on the grass.

Why was everyone behaving so strangely today?

Hwa Su did not like to be left with secretaries and officials and palace women. He liked to be with the horsemen and the archers, who were simple brave honest men and did not speak riddling nonsense.

When would he waken again to the trumpet sounding at the barracks gate? Perhaps next week, when the king returned.

Hwa Su entered the peacock door of the palace. He saw that the First Secretary and the Second Secretary and the court poet were making bundles in the corridor: the richest silk hangings and golden cups, and the jade dragons that had stood for a hundred years and more in the alcoves, and vases and plates – things that certainly did not belong to them.

'What are you doing?' said Hwa Su.

The courtiers looked up at him and their hands worked busier than ever among those rich things, arranging them hurriedly and tying the bundles with leather thongs.

'Your majesty,' said the First Secretary, 'we are going on several separate journeys. We have to pay our way.'

The court poet ripped a tapestry from the wall and stuffed it into his bundle.

Hwa Su said, 'These beautiful things belong to my father. They have belonged to the palace always. My father will not be pleased when he comes back tomorrow or the next day.'

The Second Secretary said, 'Your majesty, the trifles belong to you. You will not grudge us these few things. We have been loyal servants here this long while. Better that cultured men like us should have them than that they should be pawed and torn and squabbled over by barbarians.'

Then the three court officials shouldered their packs and staggered out with them to the courtyard, where a gilded coach and two horses and a coachman were waiting.

'This,' said Hwa Su, 'is the very strangest day of my life.'

Was it a dream? What kind of strange fantasy was being enacted in the palace? He wandered through many rooms. All were empty. A few had been stripped of their best hangings and ornaments. The hundred courtiers had stolen away silent, it seemed, and rich.

At the end of a long corridor, Hwa Su heard sounds even more terrible than the death song of the flute in the garden: grief and desolation from many mouths. This was a part of the palace he had never set foot in before: it led to the Chamber of the Queen.

Hwa Su opened the door at the end of the corridor. Inside all the women of the palace were gathered, in a disordered chaos of weeping. But when they saw Hwa Su, those who had combed his hair yesterday and those who had given him sweets and those who had measured him for a new silk coat, all the women rose and bowed with streaming faces and murmured 'majesty'.

Then, once more, they abandoned themselves to grief.

Further on, in a room in the very heart of the palace, Hwa Su (opening the door) saw a tall beautiful masked woman looking at her reflection in a mirror. She was dressed from head to foot in black.

'Who are you?', said Hwa Su. 'What is happening in this kingdom at all? I don't understand a thing.'

'What has happened,' said the masked woman, 'is an old story. War. Conquest. Defeat. It has happened a thousand times. It is the story of mankind. The same old blood-stained tear-stained page is read, over and over and over, and re-enacted. Some day the finger of history may turn the page. On the next page, it may be, there will be a beautiful thing written.'

'I do not understand,' said Hwa Su.

The masked lady said, 'Your father the king and his army were defeated at the delta three days ago, in a storm of swords. Your father the king was killed. You are king now, but for a day only, Hwa Su, until the foreign army from the delta comes with torches and warrants and daggers.'

Hwa Su began to weep.

The lady said, 'The faithful servants of your father have stripped the palace of everything beautiful and good. They have all ridden away.'

Hwa Su wept.

'There is one very old precious thing left,' said the tall lady in black, 'this golden plate. It is the most beautiful thing in the kingdom. Take it, your majesty, and go. Go at once. There is a horse waiting outside for you. I have seen to that. Ride as far from this place as you can, westwards. If they find you they will butcher you.'

'What shall I do with the gold plate?' said Hwa Su, his face all silvered with tears.

'Do something that's never been done before,' said the lady. 'Give it to some poor child. Gold and emerald and pearl, they ought to belong to all the people of the world. The rich keep them hidden away in vaults. Give that royal plate to the poorest child you can find on your travels. Go now, quickly.'

Hwa Su took the fine gold plate and put it inside his tunic.

'Who are you?' said Hwa Su. 'You speak so wisely and beautifully.'

'I'm your mother, boy,' said the masked woman in the long silk gown of death. 'I'll wait here for the barbarians. It will be an honour to die from the same edges that killed the king, my lord, your father. That way, I will be with the king tonight – I don't know where – but in a place beyond blood and scheming and gold. . . . Hurry, I hear the bridle ringing outside.'

When Hwa Su on horseback looked round, after sunset, from the mountain path, he saw far below that his beautiful palace had been caught in a net of flames.

Even the fishing boats on the river bank were little crescents of fire.

The king, Hwa Su, turned his horse's head into the sunset and the last red rocks and the huge desert beyond.

Above, a first faint star began to beat.

THE SECOND MAGUS

A drum beat, deep in the forest.

A throb then, answering, a more distant drum.

A pulse, a tremor, a faintest displacement in the blocks of darkness. Near and far, again and again, drums. The jungle was alive with drums.

The animals were in flight. Scattered plungings, crashings. The animals fled outwards to the fringes of the forest. They fled far from the drums.

The feet of the hunters and herdsmen drew, subtly, to one place. The drum beat like the heart of the forest. The beasts fled still. The people came together, in the darkness, summoned. From near and far they came, black on the blackness.

A monkey screamed and swung overhead, up and on, and was silent. Yellow eyes of a great cat shone, passing through.

Drums drove, drums lured. The forest shook with the pulsing arteries of drums. The night lived because of the drums. The large stars beat with the beat of the drums.

The largest of the stars was there, earth-rooted in the forest, suddenly. It flickered and flared and flowered. A thick lustrous hand held it high. The torch showed a hundred eyes. The torch threw dapplings over dark shoulders and thighs. Eyes and teeth shone.

The torch showed a rock and two separate shadows.

The animals had reached places of safety. The living forest belonged to the people only. It belonged to those who had small need of stars at the time of assembly. It belonged to the summoner and the summoned, the whole tribe.

A dozen torches defined the place of assembly. The many heads faced inward, eyes and teeth flashing. Men and women and children were there, the entire people. At the centre of the ring of assembly, on a rock, sat a boy. At the boy's shoulder stooped a very old man.

The drums stopped beating, all at once. The forest was possessed with a shock of silence.

More and more torches came, with people. The crowd thickened about the assembly-place. None spoke. Not even a woman spoke. No child laughed or wailed. They were struck through with the silence, an expectancy and a promise.

Behind the thick trunks, shadows moved. A carved leopard mask moved, a carved crocodile turned, a carved flamingo shook awkward wings. Maskers, they waited.

In rhythms of silence, that echoed the drums, the people waited.

The old man at the rock sang in a weak cracked voice. 'Listen. Look. All this folk, agree now together. . . .' He put his hand on the boy's shoulder. 'This is the man. This is your new chief.'

At once the people shouted together. The torches shook. A single drum pulsed, a black star, across the place of assembly.

The boy whispered, 'I am your chief.'

The old man sang, 'We must make peace again with all things. We must ask pardon of the animals. They must forgive our spears. They must forgive our nets. They must forgive our arrows. They must forgive our fires. Our hands are cunning, but they are splashed with the blood of the beasts. Our minds stink with guile and deceit.'

There was a long silence.

The boy said, in a sweet pure treble, 'I am the chief. I ask pardon of the great beautiful cats.'

A leopard mask stirred behind the trunk. It came slowly into the torch-light. The man masked as 'leopard' passed through the torchlight. In a slow stealthy crouch he approached the boy and the old man at the rock. The leopard hesitated, crouched, tilted his mask. A rustle of terror went through the people. A torch dripped blood. The leopard came then and laid its masked terror athwart the smiling head of the boy. The heads looked beyond each other into a region of peace, a separate segment of the one great circle of reconciliation.

'The animals have forgiven us,' creaked the voice of the old man, going up and down.

The drum pulsed, a black star.

The leopard masker moved back from the chief. He turned. He went, turning in a slow graceful dance, through the torches and on into the darkness beyond.

The mime of the animals went on all night. The old man sang a recital of the dreadful necessary things that the people had done to this creature and that. The people waited. The chief asked forgiveness then, each time, on behalf of the whole people. One after the other the animals came, hovered, threatened, kissed, departed with beautiful dances. The torch-lit faces flashed with joy.

Flamingo came and went. Crocodile came and went. River-fish came and went. Bat came and went. Termite came and went. All the animals returned peace to men for the evils that men had put on them.

It was a beautiful ceremony. Teeth flashed here and there with happiness.

The boy enacted the ceremony with a purity that had never been seen before. It was all the more wonderful in that the boy had never hunted and wounded and killed. The former chiefs that the people remembered had brought red hands and scarred thighs to the ceremony. Their beseeching voices had been gray with experience.

The sweet high voice pleaded, promised, blessed.

The last creature passed with the blessing beyond the torches.

After the Peace of the Animals, the drums began again, quick broken throbbings, as if the forest was in a fever.

The old man had gone back among the people and the trees. The boy sat alone against the rock.

All the torches were beaten out, like firefly swarms, except one. Now the chief and the warriors and the women would know, soon enough, how things would go with them in time unborn. Dared they raid into the marshes of the river people? Must they dig pits and raise sharp inclined posts against the people of the mountain, who had taken a dozen goats in the dark of the last moon? Would the sickness come again on their cattle? – must the pasture be shifted to the other side of the river where the hosts of blue flies did not come, on account of cold airs?

They were to learn these things, and other matters unknown and unexpected, soon.

Mobo, the young man, snarer of birds, came and stood alone in the clearing.

The looker into the womb of time stood, blind face beside the torch, tranced. The drums beat. The drums prodded him and thrashed him out of his quiet dream. A single drum beat, the drum bludgeoned him out of serenity. The man trembled. He moaned. He made a few broken steps across the clearing. He cried out in awe. He covered his eyes. He was flung to the ground. His arms and his legs twitched violently. His body shivered. The drums had put great spasms on the seeker into time. He groaned. His back was vested in silver tissue of sweat.

'This does not seem good,' said the old man to the one torch-bearer. 'I have not seen the like of this before. I do not like it. That twitching means evil. It should be a dance without staggers and spasms. The drums should stop beating. The torches should be lit again. Let the drums stop! Then the dancer will wake up. The evils will not touch us.'

'Be silent! Be silent!' cried the people.

'Let the dance go on, whatever happens,' said the small sweet voice from the rock.

'No,' said the old man stubbornly. 'I do not like this. I have never seen this before. Most years he sings. Last time his mouth was full of laughter. He danced. Wake him up.'

The seeker lay on the ground. His body shone with sweat. His flesh behaved as though it was covered with feeding ants. Half his face was teeth.

'There should be no interruptions,' said the chief. 'Even from an old wise one. What is to happen, it must be endured.'

The old one, chidden, crept back into the shadows.

The dancer rose slowly to his feet. The drums hesitated. He turned himself round, against the sun. His face was covered with his stretched hands.

'The stench!' he cried. 'The horror of rot that is to come upon this people. Death and exile. Across a great water, pain and sorrow without end. Ai! Ai!'

'Who is to do this thing to us?' said the chief. 'Is it the mountain people?'

'People we have not seen. People in long thin coats. People who are ashamed of the beauty of their bodies. People who hate the beauty of animals. These are the people who will destroy us. They will take us into distant places, across a wide wide water. A sweet smell rises now from this people to the sky. We keep the ancient fragrance in an ivory box in the chief's house. There will be no sweet smell soon. There will be a stench, worse than a rotting lion, where this people live. Stench everywhere, where the evil things are done. Stench and rottenness in the hearts of men, that can do such things. It is far off, but it will come. Let the box be carried to a place where the sweetness will cure all wounds. Ai! Ai!'

The turning body of the dancer stilled. A single tremulous drum urged him. The torch flashed full in his face. He shuddered. His features relaxed. The cords that jerked his body fell slack. The dreamer opened his eyes. He looked around him. He held up his hand slowly to the boy at the rock. He laughed. He was, again, Mobo the good snarer of birds.

'Well,' said Mobo, 'what is to happen? What came out of my stupid mouth this time? Must we sharpen our spears against the thieves from the mountain?'

Then he said, 'Why are you all looking at me with bulging eyes? I am Mobo. I catch birds. I would not harm a hair of your heads.'

Many of the people had sifted away, subtly, among the shadows. What was, most years, a long night of rejoicing and poems and flowers, was guttering out in disbelief and rage and silence. The drums were covered.

The one torch-bearer suddenly smashed his flame against the trunk. The torch went out in a thousand flung sparks and a smell of ash and resin.

'I must have said an evil thing,' said Mobo the bird-man. 'My stupid mouth!'

The old man stood again at the stone. 'Mobo should have been woken up,' he whispered. 'Then we would have been a happy people till the evil time came. To every people there comes, at last, the evil time.'

'Go,' said the chief. 'Leave me here. I will sit at the rock till morning.'

He got to his feet at last when there was one star left in the sky.

In the morning the people found that their boy chief had gone away, alone, along the forest tracks. He had taken the ivory box of incense with him.

THE THIRD MAGUS

The sun was old and sick and frail. The great golden hunter who had been the unsleeping lord of the north knocked now for shelter on the low horizon. The north opened a gray door. The sun limped through. The door closed.

Winter, a three-month darkness, closed over the peoples of the ice.

The boy raised his hand, a shadow, in farewell. A coldness touched his heart – a suspicion that this winter might be no feast of fires and flames but an endless time of ice and darkness, hunger and death.

That was nonsense. The sun always came back. After the long winter the sun came back as a bright child, cradled on the southern horizon. It grew swiftly in power and beauty. Its arrows scattered the wolf packs of winter. Soon a jar of oil stood brimming in every door.

A mystery of death and birth was enacted deep under the horizon.

The boy turned his face towards the cluster of igloos.

His mother was lighting a lamp. Now, for three months, the

lamps and candles would never be out. Over the fire crouched his father, the chief.

This was the legend.

The old sick sun goes in search of the well of renewal. All winter, withered and lost, he seeks it. He finds it at last. He drinks. Then one day he looks at the village across the rim of ice, a new bright child.

The story-teller enchanted the people still with the old story.

But in the past winter or two the young hunters had altered the central image of the legend. It had been a difficult time, many wounds one summer in the snow – wolf-fang, bear-claw. Some hunters had taken their wounds back to the fires and died. Next winter were suffering and death of another kind – hunger, sickness, a slow squandering of the people's strength.

Now, beyond the fire of the story-teller, the legend concerned blood, not water.

It was blood that renewed the winter sun: blood of the creatures, blood of the hunters. The sick sun drank from that red horn. He returned to the people, a young fierce god of spears and arrows.

In the house of the story-teller, a voice.

'There is night. Then there is morning. There is winter. Then the sun comes back. There is death, but there is a crib in the house as well as a bier, a new breath next the fire and the oil jar.

'All things return.

'Time passes, time rounds out. We are enclosed in a circle of peace.

'The circles go on, go on. But there may be an end. Somewhere there may be a break in a circle. The jars of oil have never been so low in this village. This winter, it may be, the old kind sun will have trouble finding the well.'

An old man said, 'It doesn't matter. I've had my day.'

Another old man said, 'I ate a piece of the greatest blue whale that was ever taken on this coast. I was a boy then. Two fruitful women have loved me. I once killed a man in the next village over a disputed dog. I killed him with a knife, quickly. Why should I complain if this is the last winter?'

A young man said, 'Blood-of-hunting – that is what changes the old withered sun into the young strong god. Mixed blood of the whale and the whale-man. Let the sun drink plenty of that. He will keep his tryst with us.'

A fourth man said, 'Last winter or not, there will come an end of this village soon. There are too many feeble ones here, not enough hunters and children. The chief has gray hairs. A tusk or a blocked vein will kill him some day. Who is to guard us then? There is this son of his, the thing that sits and dreams beside the fire. The one that is never out of the carver's shop. Will a few carvings save us when the men from Seal Island come against us? There have never been fewer hunters here. The men of Seal Island are very numerous now. They want our fishing holes. They have stopped trading with us. Two years now they have given us cold faces.'

An old man laughed. 'Tell us something happy. Tell the story of the girl who fell in love with the snow-goose.'

The story-teller cleared his throat. The men clapped their hands.

The boy went into the hut of the bone-carver. The bone-carver said, 'You are not to come here. Your mother has been to see me. You have to learn hunting. You have to learn how to fight and kill in the snow. You have to learn all that, not how to carve pieces of bone. You are the chief's son. You have to learn how to talk craftily in the assembly of the many villages, to friends and enemies.'

The boy said, 'I will be a carver.'

The man gave him a whale bone and a knife.

*

The great darkness made a quickening circle of hunger about land and sea, animals and people and birds and fish. The sea froze over. The sky was a wheel of flashing unsetting stars. The oil sank low in the jars.

The boy said one day to the bone-carver, 'What if the sun doesn't return? I stood in the door of the story-teller. Silence would have been better than some of the black words that were spoken.'

The bone-carver said, 'You shouldn't listen to those old fools. The sun always comes back.'

The boy said, 'What if the well is dry? The old sun king comes to the place. He dips his horn, at the solstice, into darkness and emptiness.'

'Pay attention to your work,' said the bone-carver. 'Never think of such a thing. Look, I have carved a walrus on this spear, and a hunter. On this spear, a caribou and a hunter. On this spear, a cod and a hunter. On this, a whale and many hunters. In every carving, the creature bows to the strength and cunning and hunger of the hunter. These are not decorations – I have carved a spell on every weapon. The hunters will drag the dead animals back to the fires. The village will eat and feast the winter out. Then one day (sucking the grease from their fingers) they will look up and they will see the first glow in the south. They will cover their eyes with tsin fingers. They will laugh.'

'Last winter six hunters hied by fang or tusk,' said the boy. 'It may be your spells have t ld their power.'

His mother's voice cried outside, 'Where is he? Where is that boy? Is he in your house, carver? Kick him out. Useless creature that he is! His father wants him. He is to go to the bear hunt in the morning. They know where the bear is, at last. He is in that cave under the Black Mountain.'

*

The bear stood erect outside the cave, under a half moon. The bear looked curiously at the spear in his side. He turned and looked sleepily at the circle of men. A man stepped forward and hurled another spear at the bear. It entered the bear's shoulder and hung there, quivering.

The man who had thrown the spear stepped back into the circle of hunters.

A spear was put in the boy's hand. He looked at it uncertainly. He stepped forward. He levelled the spear. The moon shone whitely along the shaft of the spear.

Suddenly the bear became conscious of the pain inside him. He raised his head. He roared. He stumbled towards the circle of hunters.

'Now,' said the chief.

The boy closed his eyes and threw the spear. He turned and ran. The circle of the hunters was broken. The bear lurched after this man and that. Heavy drops of blood scattered from the three wounds on to the snow. The boy turned again. He saw that his spear hung from the bear's belly, at an awkward angle. His hand was warm and dark with a splash of blood.

'Well done,' cried his father.

The young hunter called Ikk fell in the snow. The bear towered over Ikk. The paw of the bear slashed at Ikk. Ikk cried out. He got to his feet and ran behind the rock.

The bear had now three flashing stars of pain in his body. He roared terribly. He came down on all fours. The ice drove the spears deeper into his body. The wounds spouted blood. The hunters could hear the blood splashing on to the snow.

'Sleep, bear,' said the boy's father, the chief. 'It is time for you to have the very long sleep.'

But the bear had never been more intensely awake. He roared. He roamed here and there inside the circle of hunters. His clenched teeth shone in the moon. His unsheathed claws glittered. He stopped. He turned. He ran at the chief, the lodged spears clattering over the ice.

'Welcome, friend,' said the chief. 'I am glad you have chosen me to visit. Throdd or Grull might have run.'

The chief stepped aside. The bear blundered on. The chief turned and sank a knife into the bear's nape. Through fur and hide and bone the knife went. It snapped at once the bear's thread of life. Without a sound the creature stopped, shivered, fell over on the ice. The ice shook.

'Sleep now,' said the chief. 'You have had a good life, Grokkle. The long sleep now.'

Then the circle of hunters fell on the still-warm creature with their knives. They stripped the fur from him, with cunning swift incisions and divestings. They cut through the neck; the great head lay like a rock under the moon. A large knife scored the belly. The guts of the bear slurped and reeked over the ice. A warm stench rose from the red glistering heap.

The boy turned away. He covered his face with his hands.

The knives rasped and sang. Very soon the quartered bear was stowed on the three sledges. Far off the village dogs, smelling the blood, barked.

The hunters hitched the sledge ropes to their shoulders.

Ikk said, 'I can't pull. My shoulder is dead from the bear's claw.'

'Sit in the sledge,' said the chief. 'The boy will pull.'

'What will become of me?' said Ikk. 'I think my arm is half torn off. How will I be able to fish and hunt with one arm?'

The sledges creaked and surged on over the ice, toward the village.

'Useful things can be done with one arm,' said the chief. 'Don't think about the wound. Do you want to sit useless in the house of the old men before your time? One arm can fish. One arm can kill a man. One arm can touch a girl's hair. Be glad of the one arm.'

But suddenly the cold of the moon entered Ikk's wound through the thick fur.

The single black star of his scream was heard in the village, among the cooking fires and the growling dogs and the carved bones.

Far back, under the Black Mountain, at the opening of a cave, the spirit of the great bear lingered, amazed.

'Your face is as thin and white as an old moon,' said the carver. 'What's wrong? I hear that you did well at the bear hunt. The people are glad.'

'That bear was my brother,' said the boy.

'That bear,' said the carver, 'will sweeten the winter for us all. Out of death comes life. That is the one law that never changes.'

'I will not have it!' cried the boy. 'The bear was beautiful. I said to myself, when it came out of the cave, *I am glad to be a fellow-creature with you, Grokkle the bear*. Then we killed it, with slow mockery and rage. I threw the spear that went into its belly.'

'You did well,' said the carver. 'The hunters are singing your praises.'

'Look,' said the boy. 'The bear's blood is on my hand.'

'The old sun is smelling the blood on your hand this very morning,' said the carver. 'The new sun, when he comes, will kiss first of all the blood from the hand of the young chief.'

'It is the hand that carves,' said the boy. 'The hand that killed Grokkle is the hand that tries to make mysterious beautiful things on bone.'

'No more,' said the carver. 'Never again. Your father has been to see me. You have done your last carving. Your father has other skills to teach you. He thinks, after he is dead, you will be a great chief in this place.'

'I will make one last carving,' said the boy.

*

The boy chose the smoothest piece of ivory, a polished walrus tooth. On it he carved a man, a bear, a wolf, a skua, a caribou, a codfish, a whale. He carved that company in such a way that they seemed thirled to each other, parts of a single dance. Round this dance of the creatures he carved a simple circle.

What was the circle? It was the sun, and the Well of Renewing; it was the sign that had always surrounded the people with plenitude and peace.

The great darkness intensified.

In the house of the story-teller the ancient stories were chanted – the hunt, the battle, the voyage, the quest, the love-story.

One day the boy took his carving. He walked alone into the gray glittering wastes southward.

He never came back to the village. Years passed. He fell out of the memory of the people. 'There was once a young chief and he fell through the ice into black water and he died,' the story went.

The sun was faithful.

Time and again, year after year, the sun flashed a pure look at them across the ice rim, after the long winter. Then the people covered their eyes. They laughed. They danced.

A very old man came to the village, it's said. The doors were silent and empty. The people long since had moved on.

It was summer. The sun stood high and golden in the sky.

The old man lifted his hand to the light. His ancient face was a net of wrinkles.

Far off, the dogs smelt him. Their mouths rang like bells across the ice, a welcome.

THE FEAST AT PAPLAY

Thora, the mother of Earl Magnus, had invited both the Earls
to a banquet in Holm after their meeting on Easter Monday, and
Earl Hakon went there after the murder of the holy Earl Magnus.
Thora herself served at the banquet, and brought the drink to
the Earl and his men who had been present at the murder of her
son. And when the drink began to have effect on the Earl, then
went Thora before him and said, 'You came alone here, my lord,
but I expected you both. Now I hope you will gladden me in
the sight of God and men. Be to me in stead of a son, and I shall
be to you in stead of a mother. I stand greatly in need of your
mercy now, and I pray you to permit me to bring my son to
church. Hear this my supplication now, as you wish God to look
upon you at the day of doom.'

The Earl became silent, and considered her case, as she
prayed so meekly, and with tears, that her son might be brought
to church. He looked upon her, and the tears fell, and he said,
'Bury your son where it please you.'

Then the Earl's body was brought to Hrossey, and buried at
Christ's Kirk (in Birsay) which had been built by Earl Thorfinn.

Orkneyinga Saga

In the morning Sverr the fisherman came up from the shore to
the Hall of Paplay and called in at the kitchen door, 'Hello,
there. I have this basket of haddocks.' Gudrun the housekeeper appeared. 'Hello, Gudrun,' said Sverr. 'Here is the fish.'

'Don't take your sea-stink into the kitchen,' said Gudrun.
'Wait here at the door.'

Ingerth called from her loom, 'Who is there, Gudrun?'

'Sverr the fisherman,' said Gudrun. 'He has a basket of haddocks, lady. He wants paid for them now.'

'My mother-in-law is in the chapel,' said Ingerth. 'Tell the man he'll be paid after Mass.'

'I've a good mind to take the fish away,' said Sverr. 'Fishermen can't wait. We could easily sell them among the hill farms.'

'The lady Thora will pay you as soon as she comes in from the chapel,' said Gudrun. 'Just sit at the door for half-an-hour or so. It's Easter Monday – I hope you've been to the church yourself.'

'Some folk have to earn their living,' said Sverr sourly, and sat down on the stone at the door, beside his basket of fish.

Gudrun went back to the kitchen and sat on the fireside stool. The floor about the stool was strewn with red and white and black feathers, and from a rafter three dead naked chickens hung by their claws. Gudrun picked up a fourth chicken and began to pluck it. Feathers swirled about her feet like snowflakes. She heard someone calling outside, 'Gudrun, Gudrun, I've come with the pig. Do you want him killed now?'

It was John the herdsman. He carried a young fat placid boar under his arm.

'Yes, kill it,' said Gudrun. 'But do it away from the door. We don't want blood everywhere.'

Sverr was still sitting beside his basket of haddocks. The fish slithered feebly one on another, and gaped, and choked slowly in the dry April air.

John set the bewildered piglet on its feet in the yard. He took a knife out of his belt and pushed the blade into the pink throat. The beast squealed. It ran and staggered, and the blood welled out of it. It stood still, then shook its head in a sad puzzled way. Blood spattered on the paving-stones. The boar's eye clouded, it keeled over, and it died in floods of gore.

'It will make a very tender pork pie,' said John the herdsman.

'What's happening out there at all?' said Ingerth from her loom.

Gudrun hung the fourth chicken from the rafters by its feet. She took a straw basket from the recess and went out into the yard. The two men, Sverr and John, were playing some kind of a game on the pavement, tossing flat stones into a circle scratched on the furthest flagstone. Gudrun crossed over the field to the mill. She had to bake a great quantity of bread and cakes for the feast that evening. The two greatest men in Orkney were to be the guests at the table: the Earl Magnus (Thora's son) and the Earl Hakon. She would have to excel herself. Thank goodness, some of the farm girls would be coming in the afternoon to help in the kitchen. The ale, she thought; the ale at least will be very good. She had made it a month ago, in the cold hard air of March, always the best time for brewing. The ale had been seething gently for three weeks in barrels beside the kitchen fire. The earls would be glad of Gudrun's ale after their journey from the island, at sunset.

The little bell above the chapel at the end of the Hall began to nod and cry, and the bronze mouth brimmed with sound. *The Lord is risen! The Lord is risen! The Lord is risen!*

Ljot the stable-boy tugged at the bell-rope. The upsurge lifted him to his toes, again and again.

The Mass was over. A tall woman came out of the church, and after her a few farm women. She walked purposefully towards the door of the Hall. The priest told the stable-boy to stop ringing the bell so hard – he would have his arms out of their sockets, he would crack the bronze. The women from the farms smiled. Sverr the fisherman and John the herdsman threw their splintered stones into the grass and rose to their feet as the woman approached. 'The Lord is risen,' said the lady Thora, the widow of Erlend Earl of Orkney, to the two men. They mumbled a greeting to her. Thora passed into the Hall. 'The Lord is risen,' she said in the interior gloom and coldness.

Ingerth, working at her loom, did not reply.

Gudrun crossed back over the field from the mill carrying a basket of new meal on her shoulder. 'A good Easter to you,' she greeted the women who were returning now from the Easter service to this croft and that fishing bothy. They raised their hands and answered, 'And to you too, Gudrun.'

The lady Thora put a silver piece into the palm of Sverr's hand. 'Thank you, my lady,' said the fisherman, 'it is too much.' His tarry fist shook with greed and joy.

'No,' said Thora, 'but I have never seen such firm bright haddocks.'

Gudrun set down her oatmeal on the table. The kitchen was hot and full of the smells of blood and strangulation. The ale seethed gently in the barrels and gave out a sweet smell. Gudrun added some peats to the fire. 'Outside,' she said to the thin black cat that was stretching itself beside the new flames. Gudrun took a sharp knife and went out to the yard to gut the fish. The cat, smelling the dead salt creatures, ran after her, mewling faintly.

The Hall precincts were empty now, except for the boy Ljot who was sitting in the grass looking up at the shivering silent bell.

Gudrun listened at the door between kitchen and hall. Her mistress was saying to Ingerth, whose loom still clacked and birred inside, 'It was a beautiful Mass.'

Ingerth, her daughter-in-law, wife of Magnus the earl, said nothing.

'The Lord is risen,' said Thora in a hurt voice. 'Does that mean nothing to you? Of course it means nothing, if one does not see all the actions of Christ's life in the events of every day. Today in the island of Egilsay your husband and his cousin – the two earls – who have been on bad terms for years, they are holding a meeting. They are making a treaty. Does that mean nothing to you? Orkney that has been bleeding to death for many

winters, that is dead in fact and laid in a hollow rock, Orkney is
to be resurrected again this very day. Does that mean nothing
to you?'

'I am dead also,' said Ingerth. 'I am dead here in your house.
I lie dead every night in my bed. I think I will never come to life
again. All that talk means nothing to me.'

'The bread was broken in the church this morning,' said
Thora. 'Here, tonight, in this very room, it will be broken
again: the bread of peace. Does that not gladden your heart?'

'Nothing gladdens the heart of a married virgin who is growing old,' said Ingerth, and sent the shuttle flying again with
fierce clackings.

Soon, from the kitchen fire, came the smell of baking bread.

Five farm girls came in the afternoon to help Gudrun in the
kitchen and the house. One swept the floor of the main chamber;
one scrubbed the great table; one ran and fetched for Gudrun, a
little salt from the stone in the cupboard, a few dock-leaves from
the ditch to keep the fish cool; one watched the fire anxiously,
bringing in peats from time to time and stirring the flames;
Solveig would have been better biding at home – she stood
between the hearth and the kitchen bench gossiping like a bird
all afternoon, yet Gudrun did not reprove her because it was
such a special day: Easter Monday, and in the evening, here in
Holm, the feast of the reconciled earls.

The girls murmured and giggled to each other from time to
time, passing with broom or salt or flame or fish-oil.

'. . . and so I just said to him,' said Solveig. '"Peter," I said,
"you needn't bother coming back here, I don't want to see you
again, what about the silver ring I gave you, what about my three
pearls found in the oysters, what have you done with them,
drunk them most like, now I know it only too well, you've been
coming here all winter to this house for only one thing, but now

I've had enough, you can go some other place, what do you take me for, a simpleton," I said. And the last I saw of him he was going round the corner of the pigsty like a kicked dog, but the ale-house had the story the same night, and the brute was getting pots of beer for telling it over and over again. . . .'

'I am glad to be here today,' whispered little Una to the lady Thora as she passed her in the main doorway. Una was carrying in bits of greenery for the garnishing of the fish once they were baked.

'It is Easter again,' said Thora to herself as she walked in her thick coat through the fields towards the shore. 'The whole world is alive and astir with resurrection. Look at the new grass in the ditch, how young it is and full of sap, and the wild flowers everywhere, and the birds dropping back among the islands from the fires of Africa.'

She passed some peat-cutters, a man and two women, on the hill. 'Bless your ladyship,' said the women humbly as the lady of the Hall went past, but the man turned his back and sank his blade viciously into the soft spongy turf. 'Get on with your work,' he whispered to the women. 'Do you want to be warm next winter? It's all right for her – she gets her peats cut and dried for her, yes, and set on the fire, yes, and the ashes raked in in the morning. She can walk about in the sun if she wants to. But the likes of us, we have to work our guts out for everything we have. . . .' He spat on his hands. The two women clucked at him reprovingly.

'The very light is renewed at this time of year,' said Thora to herself as she walked on towards the shore. 'The air is no longer shroud-grey. There's a brightness in the wind. And the stars are not so fierce as in winter. There's a sweetness in that great wheel as it goes through the sky on an April night.'

A man ploughing behind an ox in the field below raised his

hand and shouted, 'A good Easter, my lady,' Thora stopped and answered, 'And to you too,' and passed on down to the beach where a few fishermen were sitting beside their sheds working with hooks and creels. . . . Behind her, in a fold of the hills, Tolk the ploughman fell to cursing at his ox; but even the cursings sounded new-minted, and they diminished at last to a few remote bright fragments.

Thora stood with her feet among the weeded washed rocks. At her approach the fishermen had turned their backs, not out of discourtesy but because they were shy in the presence of the great lady. They knitted their creels and baited their lines with great concentration. A lamb fluttered among the dunes; the ewe called to it from the edge of a low crag.

'At this time of year,' said Thora to herself, 'new life appears everywhere on the earth – lambs, calves, grice, nestlings. The new creatures come trooping through the door of summer. Heaven has ordained everything with great wisdom. Only man, the prodigal, is littered at all seasons of the year. How strange that is. Christ, as if to emphasise his manhood, chose to place his death at this time of birth and quickening; but at once, three days afterwards, he asserted his godhead by bringing out of death this thing that is so much more marvellous than birth even – resurrection. The whole earth and sea today is shaken with resurrection. . . . Halcro,' she called to the oldest fisherman, 'thank you for the haddocks. Sverr brought them to the Hall. They are good fish. A good Easter to you all. I am expecting Earl Magnus and Earl Hakon from Egilsay round about sunset.'

'They will come by road, my lady,' said Halcro. 'I hear there are horses waiting on the shore at Tingwall.'

That, thought Thora, was how they would come indeed. She was standing among her fishermen at one end of this large island that was called the Island of Horses – Hrossey. Earl Magnus and Earl Hakon would, after their kiss of peace on the island of Egilsay, cross over in a small boat to the shore of Tingwall.

Their squires would have been waiting since morning with the horses. Tingwall and Paplay were at opposite ends of the Island of Horses. The earls would have a long ride from Tingwall to the shore of Firth, then across the flank of Wideford Hill to the village of Kirkwall with its little church of St. Olaf. They would stop there most likely for refreshment – a cup of wine and some honeyed bread – with the priests, then on again along the sea-banks above Scapa Flow, until in the thickening light they saw below them the Hall of Paplay with its festive lights and flames.

'There will be happiness in Orkney now,' said Thora to the old man.

Alternatively the two earls might sail from Egilsay, past the flat island of Wyre, then between Gairsay with its one hill and the long sprawl of Shapinsay, and avoiding Kirkwall and the priests sail through The String and drop anchor in the sheltered bay at Inganess. There they could get horses at a farm, and ride between the heather and the little bird-haunted hill lochs. In either case, the final stage of the journey would have to be by horse.

The lady Thora thought for a while, between the shining April sea and the ploughlands, of the skill and toughness and patience of the island generations. Hundreds of years ago men had come hungry to these islands, easterlings, and they had hauled up their longships here and at a score of other bays and inlets, and they had turned their salt sinewy hands to the earth. They had hewed cornerstones and set them here and there along the shore. They had dug little fields out of the heather. In summer they turned their axes against the dark folk who lived among the hills. Harvests came, a good one this year, an indifferent one that year; and their beasts multiplied and their beasts dunged the earth and their beasts were struck down before winter. The families made alliances, quarrelled, schemed; and love blossomed here and there, erratic and marvellous. Somehow that Scandinavian tribe learned to live at reasonable peace, the farmer on the hill with the farmer at the loch-side (though the women at the hearths were forever stirring up jealousies and ambitions and old angers). Or if a field here or there was desperately disputed, the litigants took it to the district assembly, and generally abode by the verdict of the men sitting solemnly on the side of the little hill. There were occasional spear-storms and corn-batterings; but in spite of that life had gone on, with new fields dug out of the hill year after year, and new poems sung to the harp, and new innocent eyes opening to the sun. There was a feeling of slow continuous ripening, generation by generation, as of corn wavering sunwards through a long summer of history. The time of the great Earl Thorfinn – grandfather of Magnus and Hakon – seemed now, looking back, like a golden harvest, with all the sanctity and song and heroism that were in the islands at that time.

After the death of Earl Thorfinn it was as if a chill wind blew in from the sea, and the sun shrank. The horses reared their hooves at the gray sun beyond the equinox. Winter came early with its frosts and fires; that is to say, looking at these matters in the long perspective of history, for the past two generations life in the islands had not been so agreeable as it had been up to then. Spite, anger, upset in every island, in every district, in every household – a sense of stagnation and loss, of a honeycomb broken and the sweetness draining away.

What had happened? Some argued that it was simply a loss of independence and identity. The king of Norway had asserted all too successfully his overlordship of the islands (as he had not dared to do in Earl Thorfinn's time), and to emphasize it had set up two puppet earls to squeak and gesture at each other; for he knew that a single strong ruler in Orkney could, with a cynical half-nod eastwards, plough his own furrow and fill his own barns. So much was true: the lady Thora knew well enough how it had been with her own husband Erlend, yoked impotently in the earldom along with his brother Earl Paul. In those days the yawls had begun to rot along the shore. But matters had got much worse under the double rule of Magnus Erlendson and Hakon Paulson – war had broken out – all Orkney was sundered into two hostile camps, and foreign mercenaries rode through the cornfields all one summer – there was everywhere a sense of hopelessness and futility.

If misfortune goes on for too long – if stones drift over the mouth of springs and people no longer have the will to shift them – then one has a sense of other than purely political forces at work; a veiled mysterious cipher has entered the equation; Fate has taken a hand in the game.

As year on year of murder and bad faith and anarchy succeeded one another, it seemed that an evil winter indeed was deepening over everything. The islanders trembled at the approach of the black solstice. They knew well enough in theory how the disorder could be cured: if they had a single strong earl standing in the door of his palace up there in Birsay, guarding the heraldry and the music and the lawbook and the looms inside.

But now events had passed out of their control. They could do nothing about the evils all around them. Fate was working out its own dark inscrutable design, which seemed to be the death of Orkney. The mere mention of the word 'Fate' increased the hopelessness and helplessness.

Indeed (thought Thora as she walked back home through the fields) the ancient faith continues to be strong here in the north. Men acquiesce too easily still in the orderings of Fate. They have had Christianity for more than a hundred years and they are not comfortable with the new religion. It has not entered into the bloodstream of the tribe at all. Well, today in Egilsay, the new faith was being put to the test. The Orkneymen would see soon enough what a miraculous strength would flow from this meeting of enemies in Egilsay. It would be finally proven to them that it is Christ that rules the universe, not Fate.

Even a pagan might feel on a day like this that the islands were astir with hope and expectation and promise. The Lord is risen. The dove is fallen and furled in Egilsay now, thought Thora. The meeting is over. The horsemen are on the road to Paplay.

As she drew near the Hall she saw two of the farm girls – Gudrun's helpers – bringing the slaughtered piglet from a hook on the courtyard wall to the fires inside. The beast had a dark gash at its throat. . . .

At the shore, the crew of *Godspell* still sat among the creel-stones and twine. It was the first afternoon that year that they had been able to sit out of doors.

'She's a good kind lady,' said Old Halcro reverently. 'God help her.'

'A fine sight it'll be,' said his son Harald, 'the two earls on the road, and all the gentry of Orkney riding behind them. From the ale-house door we might get a glimpse of them.'

'There'll be music and feasting till all hours,' said another fisherman.

'I'll tell you what the best sight of all would be,' said a young fisherman called Ward. (His father had lost all his fields and his steading in the troubles, and Ward had had to beg the fishermen for a place in their boat.) 'I'll tell you what the best sight of all would be – one horseman on the road tonight, a hard solitary silent man.'

The fishermen looked at Ward and shook their heads. They did not know what he was talking about.

In the Hall kitchen the preparations were almost over. There was a heap of baked haddocks on a platter at one side of the fire; on the other the huge pot of chicken broth steamed. One of the girls turned the young pig on the spit. The first of the ale had been poured into a silver jug and it had a tilted cap of froth. Gudrun's face was flushed. The lady Thora entered from the main chamber. Her hair hung loose. Some new idea must have occurred to her in the middle of her toilet.

The sun had been down over Hoy for ten minutes or more.

'Solveig', said Thora, 'you've done little but chatter nonsense all day. Go out and listen for the sound of hooves. They'll be riding between Gaitnip and Deepdale. It's a calm evening. You'll be able to hear them miles off.'

Solveig put on her shawl and went outside.

The pig on the spit rained drops of its own burning fat into the fire.

'Una,' said Thora, 'have you set the ale-horns, a dozen of them, on the table?'

'Yes, I have,' said Una, 'and I polished the silver bits round the rims too.'

'Well, don't stand there gaping – carry the goblet through,' said Thora.

From the main chamber came the slow irregular clack of the shuttle. The lady Ingerth had been at her weaving all day, and still she sat at the loom in the fading light, plotting intricacies of form and colour. She mingled scarlet thread with black thread and gray thread. It was uncertain yet what the web was meant to represent.

'The priests in Kirkwall are keeping them,' said Thora. 'That's what it is. Meantime the fish is getting cold. Magnus said they would be here before sundown, for sure. . . . Gerda.'

'Ma'am,' said Gerda.

'Go out and stand on the howe. You have good eyesight. See if you can see them.'

'It's getting dark, ma'am,' said Gerda.

'Just do what I say,' said Thora. 'Keep your eyes on the road. If you keep looking you'll see a thicker moving clot of shadows on the hillside. That will be them.'

Gerda took her flushed face into the darkening wind outside.

'There's two or three good ale-houses between Tingwall and here,' said Gudrun, between innocence and mockery.

'Earls are not blacksmiths and poachers,' said Thora. 'Earls don't go into ale-houses.'

Solveig Rattle came back out of the night, shivering. 'There's no sound of horses on the road at all,' she said. 'I crouched there five minutes with my ear to the ground.'

The loom fell silent next door.

'I've heard,' said little Una to Broda, breaking the new bread with her fingers and arranging the pieces on a platter, 'I've heard that Earl Hakon is a terrible man. Of course I've never really set eyes on him. But they say he's fierce and black as a wolf.'

'That's nonsense, Una,' said Thora. 'Earl Hakon is a very gentle courteous person. You'll see that for yourself before the night's done. Broda, my hair.'

'Maybe, Una,' said Solveig, 'he'll take you on his knee.'

'O for the love of God,' shrieked Una. 'I would die!'

Gerda came back, cold and gray-faced. She squatted beside the fire and held her hands out to the blaze. 'The road's empty, ma'am,' she said. 'There's nothing moving in the darkness but a cow and a few fishermen going from the beach to the ale-house.'

'It could be,' said Gudrun, 'that the meeting took longer than they thought. Maybe they didn't get away from Egilsay till late.'

Broda stood on tiptoe behind Thora. She pushed the comb into the burnished coils of hair and fastened it with a pin.

'That's possible,' said Thora. 'That's likely, in fact. They were hard and difficult, the things they had to discuss. If only Magnus and Hakon had been there themselves, the two of them, it would all have been so much more simple. But there were men in Egilsay today – Sighvat Sokk for example, and Hold Ragnarson – awkward difficult creatures at any time – supposed to be councillors – they couldn't counsel a cock to crow. . . .'

'There will be a wish-bone for everybody,' said Gudrun to Una and Broda. 'Don't quarrel about it.'

Through the open kitchen door the first star shone above the hill.

'Whatever delay there has been,' said Thora, 'Magnus and Hakon are coming to Holm. Nothing will stop them. It was a promise. They'll come, I know it. They'll come if it should be midnight.'

'This pig will be a cinder long before midnight,' said Gudrun. She took her forearm across her shining brow.

The dog set up a sudden fearful unending hullabaloo at the gate: until the stable-boy ran out and silenced him.

'Listen,' said Una.

The women stood about the open door. They tilted their heads. They touched their fingers to their ears. They heard breathings in the night, a distant whinny and snicker, thuds on the soft turf, the bright faint chime of harness. A troop of horsemen was abroad. A horn blew. As if the rising sea rolled stones upon rock there was a sudden outbreak of clops and splashes – the horsemen were crossing the burn half a mile away. The women heard Ljot calling, 'This way, this way – follow the lantern.' The night was one jangling snorting onset then, though the hooves fell muted again on the grass of the park: a tumult of thuds and breathings, coming closer. 'This way, my lord,' said Ljot – 'take care of the duckpond'. Iron on stone: the cobbled courtyard was loud with men and horses. 'The stable is over here,' cried Ljot. 'I'll hang the lantern in the rafters. There's plenty of hay. There's water in the trough over there.'

'It's them,' cried Solveig, clapping her hands. 'They've come!'

'Come back inside, all of you,' said Thora. 'Shut the door. Gudrun, see to the ladling of the soup. I don't want any carry-on tonight between women and horsemen. Remember what day it is. When I sound the bronze, that will be the time to put the fish on the plates. Una, come with me, please.'

Thora opened and closed the door between kitchen and hall.

Una followed her. Ingerth had left the loom and was pacing unquietly between the hearth and the table.

'Your husband is here,' Thora said. 'Get ready. I should put on something gay – that yellow gown for example....' She passed on, followed by Una, into her bed-chamber.

The clatter of hooves lessened in the courtyard as the horses were led one by one from the troughs to the flickering stable. To the girls watching from the kitchen the yard was a throng of noisy shadows. One tall shadow detached itself from the clamour. It moved, slow and hesitant, towards the stone heraldry of the main door. A fist rose and fell.

Ingerth in her sombre dress stood behind the loom and did not stir in the direction of the vibrant oak.

Thora, fixing a silver brooch to the shoulder of the red magnificence swathing her, came breathless out of her room towards the summons, followed by Una.

'Welcome,' she said. And pulled the heavy door open.

A solitary figure reeled in, and stood there, rooted, shaking his head slowly in the light. Thora and Ingerth recognized, through the ale-stupor and the mask of fatigue, Hakon Paulson, the second of the two expected guests.

'I've come, Thora,' he said. 'I'm here.'

'You're welcome, Hakon,' said Thora. She moved towards him anxiously. He bent his barley-reeking head. Thora kissed him on the cheek. 'A good Easter to Earl Hakon,' she said.

'From Egilsay to here was a long hard journey,' said Hakon thickly. 'I've had one or two rough journeys in my time. This was the worst.'

'Sit down, Hakon,' said Thora. 'You're very tired.'

Hakon took his axe from his belt and laid it on the table. He sat down with tipsy suddenness in the high chair. His face was carnival red among the torches. 'Yes,' he said, 'I'm tired. There was a lot of business to do in Egilsay today.'

'So,' said Ingerth. The shifting fire-reflections went over her

and filled with shadows her cheeks and temples and throat. Her
face fluttered slowly in the fire-and-torch-light. Her black eyes
never left Hakon's face.

'I came as quickly as I could,' said Hakon. 'We had trouble
with the horses. One cast a shoe. They turned their heads away,
anywhere but in this direction. The horses did not want to come
to Holm. One broke his leg on Wideford. They had to finish
him off.'

'Hakon,' said Thora, 'it looks to me that you've been celebrating early.'

'No,' said Hakon, 'but I do not like killing. The horse – it was
Sigurd's gelding – he stumbled on a loose stone on the side of
Wideford. We had to kill him. That kept us back.'

There was silence in the Hall. From the kitchen came the
clatter of pots and the cold swift orders of Gudrun to the farm-
girls. Little Una stood at the door between hall and kitchen,
waiting for the word to bring in the soup.

'The dinner is almost ready,' said Thora. 'You must be
hungry, Hakon.'

'No,' said Hakon. 'I want to drink.'

'Una,' said Thora, 'tell Gudrun that we do not want the soup
or the fish just yet. Tell her to fill a jug with the oldest strongest
ale – the stuff she brewed for Christmas.'

Una disappeared into the hot clattering kitchen.

'So, what is keeping Magnus so long out in the stable?' said
Thora.

Una came from the kitchen carrying the silver goblet. She set
it carefully on the table before Thora. Thora tilted the jar into
a cup. The ale went over thick and frothy and dark. She handed
the cup to Earl Hakon. 'Magnus is not in the stable,' said Earl
Hakon. 'Magnus is in Egilsay.' He drank till the beard on his
upper lip was dark and soaking. He noticed Ingerth standing
between the loom and the hearth fire. 'Madam,' he said, 'your
husband Earl Magnus is in Egilsay. Magnus couldn't come to

Holm tonight.' He drank again. 'This is very good ale,' he said.

'It is all one to me,' said Ingerth, 'where he is.'

'Una,' said Thora, 'put some more of the ale into the earl's cup.'

Una poured out of the jug. Her hands shook. The horn shook. Some ale fell on Hakon's fist.

'You stupid girl!' cried Thora. 'Have you never learned to pour straight out of a jug!'

Una's lower lip quivered and she set the empty jug on the table. 'I'm sorry,' she whispered to Earl Hakon.

'No,' said Hakon, 'but it was my arm that was shaking. What's your name, girl?'

'Una.'

'You are a very pretty girl, Una. I'm sure you're a great help to the lady Thora. It was my fist that was shaking and so some of the ale got spilled.'

'Yes, lord,' said Una.

'Una,' said Thora, 'the jug is empty. Ask Gudrun to fill it up again from the same barrel.'

'Yes,' said Una, and lifted the empty jug from the table.

'Tell Gudrun,' said Thora, 'that we will not be needing food after all. Tell her the girls are to carry the food to the men in the stables.'

'Keep coming back with the ale jug,' said Hakon. 'You are a good girl.'

'So Magnus is staying tonight in Egilsay,' said Thora.

'That's right,' said Hakon. 'In Egilsay. Magnus is staying tonight in Egilsay.'

'What house, I wonder?' said Thora. 'Will he be sleeping in some farm, or at the priest's house?'

'No house,' said Hakon. 'I wish that girl would hurry with the ale. He is spending the night in the fields.'

Una came back with the goblet and set it on the table, and stood looking with wide eyes at Earl Hakon.

'Go back to the kitchen,' said Thora sharply to Una. 'The earl and I have important things to talk about.'

'You are a very sweet pretty girl,' said Hakon. Thora poured ale into Hakon's cup. Una went back into the kitchen. Ingerth twisted her ring, a glittering golden snake-writhe on her finger: she looked at Hakon indifferently.

From the yard and the stable came sounds of laughter, a mingling of bright and dark cries. The women were offering fish and bread and cheese to the men who had ridden from Egilsay. A woman broke the chickens into hot pieces. A woman put a knife into the roast pig. There were cheers when a girl crossed the yard with her arms full of ale-horns. The horses nuzzled the hay. Solveig shrieked twice. There were volleys of dark and bright cries. The main barn of Paplay was a house of laughter.

Earl Hakon put the ale cup to his mouth and emptied it with several strong workings of his throat. 'This is very good ale,' he said. 'I congratulate you. I'll tell you something. I am not a coward but I was terrified to come to this house tonight. What were we talking about?'

'Magnus in Egilsay,' said Thora.

'Magnus is not staying in any house,' said Hakon. 'Magnus is spending the night under the stars.'

'It will be cold for him,' said Thora. 'He did not take his thick coat with him.'

'No,' said Hakon, 'he is not needing any coat. Magnus will never need another coat. But I need more ale.'

'So,' whispered Ingerth. 'It is the dark bride.'

'Hakon,' said Thora, 'I think you've had plenty of that ale. You would be better off with something to eat.'

'No meat,' said Hakon. 'I carved flesh in Egilsay today. I was hellishly sick after it.'

'Your axe is clean enough,' said Thora.

'It was Ofeig's axe,' said Hakon. 'I didn't do anything

personally, if you understand. Lifolf the cook, he did it. You know Lifolf the cook? We put Ofeig's axe into his hands. Lifolf carved the meat.'

There was another long silence in the hall: the man building round his day's work a labyrinth of drunkenness – an old woman stumbling down dark hints and guesses to a simple central event (a fire on a stone, a lustration, a dove-fall). Ingerth looked at the web in the loom. It was grey lamb's wool, lightly woven, a half-finished summer coat: that would never now be worn.

Hakon poured a cup of ale for himself with a steady hand.

'Still you haven't told me what happened in Egilsay today,' said Thora.

Hakon drank deeply.

'A man died,' he said. 'That's what happened. A man died.'

'Well,' said Thora, 'that's always happening. Men die. Never a day but a man dies in this island or that. So long as this dead man in Egilsay was shriven and given heavenly bread for his journey, then he's happy enough, I'm sure. So long as he's lying in the church in Egilsay, between the font and the altar, all's well with him. The living weep – a mother, a widow, children weep – but there's worse things than a good death.'

'There were no children in this case,' said Ingerth.

'The dead man,' said Hakon, 'he is not in the church. He is in the fields. He is lying under the stars. I told you.'

'It is a work of mercy,' said Thora, 'to give the dead sanctuary and burial. What were you all thinking of in Egilsay today? There is more ale in the jug. Were you all so busy with peace-making that you had no time to carry this poor man who died into the kirk?'

Hakon kneaded his eyes with his fists. He bent his head on the table beside the ale jug. A convulsion, like a slow ponderous wave, passed through his body, from chest to knees. His face streamed. He opened his mouth. He yelled once like a beast under a branding iron.

'Well wept, butcher,' said Ingerth.

Thora lifted one huge trembling fist from the table and stroked it. 'Well now,' she said, 'when you think of it there's worse places for a dead man to lie than the fields. But still I would be better pleased if the wounds and the silence were laid before the altar in the kirk of Egilsay. It isn't much for an old woman to ask.'

Hakon whispered that he would send word to the priest and people of Egilsay in the morning. He sat up. He said in a firm voice that he was very tired. He said he must be on his way now. He thanked them for the fire and the ale. But still he sat where he was.

Thora touched him on the shoulder. He rose blindly to his feet. She kissed him again on his shivering mouth. She lit a candle from one of the wall torches. She called him 'son'. She led him through the far door to the bed chamber beyond.

The byres and the barn and the stables round the courtyard brimmed with laughter and shouts and songs.

'The filth,' said Ingerth. 'The scum. The beast.'

On the half-finished cloth in the loom could be seen now, in the torchlight, a sun, a cornstalk, a cup.

THE DAY OF THE OX

There are months and years when nothing happens. Nothing has happened here since I was a child, such as happened in the ancient stories of the coast.

There is always a time of full nets and empty nets.

There is a laden barn or an empty barn: the worm has been at the root, sun and rain have been at odds with the green shoots, the people have made a wrong dance at midsummer round the fire on the hill. Mostly, it is a barn half-way between plenty and dearth.

But a life-relish has gone out of the people. Why? We have been at peace for a generation. No ships have sailed from the Minch with a sharp gleam here and there, at prow or amidships.

The old burnt skulls knew such disturbances. Death sometimes made itself a feast in the village – old men and children, shepherd and fisherman and ploughman, knelt and fell before the knives of the southerners. Or, some winter, a fever burned them to the skull.

Yet we have their fine songs. The poet remembers a hundred rhymes and stories out of that hard time.

For thirty years there has been no new song on this quiet coast.

One evening, just before harvest, I went with others to the chief's house. He would tell us what things were to be done in the morning – if the weather was good – into what corner the first sickle must go, which women could be spared for gleaning and the binding of sheaves. The old man pointed at me – 'You will put the sickle in first.'

Heavy with all the suns of that good summer, I must have dropped into sleep where I sat among the harvesters.

I dreamed.

A man, a stranger, came into the chief's house. He said nothing. The chief's girl took a fish from the embers and offered it to the stranger, and a piece of bread. He took the food and ate it thanklessly beside the fire. Nor did he look any man or woman in the face. The girl had blown the hearth into flames. The man took off his coat, and his arm was golden-haired, as if it was circled by a harvest wind. And then he took off his woven hat, and a torrent of hair as bright as the sun fell over his shoulders.

The girl cried out with amazement.

Having eaten and licked his fingers, the man took his coat about him and left the hut, without a word or a sign of thanks. It was as if to him we were a company of shadows.

When I woke up, the people were sitting silently round the fire in the chief's house. Usually before we go to our separate huts, the poet tells an old story. Tonight, on the eve of harvest, the Song of Bread should have been on his tongue: an old blessing, first uttered on the coast a hundred years ago. But the poet was silent. At last he said, 'I have had an evil dream. A man out of a time to come was here. He left a shadow in this house that will never go away. I am cold. I will say no more.'

The girl said, 'I have not seen a man so tall and bright and handsome. It was a dream. There are no such men in the world. I was glad to give him fish and bread in my dream.'

Some of the other villagers said that they too had fallen asleep, and dreamed of an arrogant greedy sunlike stranger.

'I dreamed the same dream,' said the chief. 'I tell you this, it was a good dream, now on the eve of harvest. Such brightness, such greed, such thanklessness. For so the elements work, in ways different from our ways. The earth takes our sweat and blood, and sometimes is generous to us, and sometimes is stingy. The sea too, it covers the shore stones with twisting silver, or else it drowns a young man in his curragh and leaves the village hungry. That's the way of the elements. As for us, in our dream we dealt courteously with the stranger, and that is how it should be, as far as we understand things. . . . That golden thankless man, I tell you, is a good augury for the harvest.'

Nothing happens along this coast. In the old days, after harvest, young men would go with knives into a boat and sail to some hidden island, where they were not known, and plunder, and come home again with pieces of silver, and blood on their daggers. But the last two generations have not known such adventure. The village has settled into a gray peace.

The dream that had come upon the village was whispered among the other villages of the coast. We suffered much mockery because of the dream. They laughed behind their hands. What kind of honey and heather ale had we drunk that night? How much extra malt had the brewing wife poured into the vat? Had there been many sore heads in our village the next morning?

'Let them mock on,' said the chief. 'The scarecrow has more understanding than them.'

It seemed that the dream was a good augury. We reaped a bigger harvest than for many years.

In the time between equinox and solstice, there was no storm or rough winds on the sea. The fishing boats came to shore day after day with torrents of living silver.

I think that that midwinter was the merriest time I had known in the village. Once or twice, the mouth of the poet trembled towards a new song, but nothing new came, only the old songs of snow and fire, darkness and drinking and beached whales.

After that solstice, the chief became very bent and gray, as if a shadow had passed into him.

But he did not die.

Winter sifted into the hut of the blacksmith, and soaked into his flesh and gnawed at his marrow; and soon Blok was a burnt skull in the cairn. A child wept for Blok at the door of the House of the Dead.

The snow of winter was at last only a streak or two on Kierfea across the Sound.

'It's time now,' said the chief in his new gray voice, 'to yoke the oxen.'

It was time to yoke the first ox and unearth the plough from the summertime debris of the barn.

The monotony of another summer was about to begin. (And why had the vanished poet, who was a charred tongueless skull in the cave, why had he made such fine songs about plough and harrow, and the dialogue of seed and the ever-brightening sun, while our poet had nothing new to say about such things, but chanted·over and over again the fire-forged and hammered words of the old poet, a tarnished hoard?)

It was appointed to me, that spring, to open the door of the byre and to say to the ox, 'Come, ox, it is time for us to work together, it is time to begin the ceremony of corn.'

Then I had to loosen the ox from his chain at the wall, and to lead him forth into the light. He was so used, the ox, to the winter dark of the byre and the lantern twice a day, that his first sight of the sun put a kind of madness on him. He pranced, he smote the air with his hoof, his tail lashed, he put down his head as if he would charge at the horizon and break it! But soon, the yoke at his neck, he grew patient again, a friend to the village and the hungers of the village.

As I led the ox to the big field, followed by a crowd of

villagers old and young, I saw the gulls rising from the crag in fierce broken circles. There had not been such rage and commotion among the cliff faces since the three whales had stranded there ten winters ago.

I topped the ridge, gently urging the ox (and the cries of the villagers behind were almost a match for the blizzarding gulls).

Below me, on the shore, stood the winter stranger – the man in the dream – and a dozen others with him. Each man carried an axe. A ship like a great hollow bird was anchored in the Sound.

I pointed.

The villagers turned. Their mouths were suddenly silent, as they were gathered into a dream they would not wake from. They bowed their heads.

The strangers stood unmoving on the shore, among axe-glitterings.

The ox turned his horns towards the destroyers. He knelt, offering them his services.

THE BATTLE IN THE HILLS
A story for women's voices

NOTE: The battle of Summerdale was fought in 1529 between a royal army recruited mainly in Caithness and Orkneymen who were in a state of rebellion against King James V.

The host met in the valley of Summerdale between Orphir and Stenness.

One old Orphir woman had been asked by the King's general, Lord William St Clair, to tell how the battle would go. She unrolled two balls of wool. She declared that the first man to be killed that day would overshadow his people – Orkney or Caithness – with certain defeat.

The only Orkneyman to die at Summerdale was mistakenly killed by his own mother, hours after the battle was over.

SIX WOMEN:
>   GUNNHILD, a croft wife
>   SOLVEIG, a croft wife
>   THORA, a croft wife
>   RAGNA, a very old woman
>   ANNA, a servant on a farm, a Caithness woman
>   INGERD, a widow with a son

[1]

(*The women come together to a green place on the safe side of the hill between Orphir and Stenness. An early morning – daybreak – in the year 1529.*)

A trumpet : followed by the voice of an unseen herald :
'The islands of Orkney within the Kingdom of Scotland is hereby proclaimed to be in a state of rebellion against us, King James the Fifth of Scotland. Wherefore we summon the lords and commons of Orkney to acknowledge the sovereignty of King James, or to have their traitorous fields and ships wrung with fire and steel: and that with the utmost suddenness, rigour, and despatch.

'God save the King!'

GUNNHILD   Yes, they did. They came ashore in the first light: hundreds of men with swords and axes: soldiers. The great one was with them, William St Clair, our expelled lord. He carried in his purse the King's commission. The army of William St Clair is to root out rebellion in Orkney today.

They stood on the Orphir shore at dawn. The soldiers of King James shouted. Their axes flashed in the new sun.

When I turned to ask my man what was going on he was not there. Sven had taken to the hills.

SOLVEIG   Listen. A movement in the hills. Many stealthy feet, coming from near and far into one place. Listen, the Orkneymen are coming together like thieves, or crows to the one darkling tree.

And my Erling is one of them: a traitor.

I am ashamed. The King is there in the city of Edinburgh to be honoured and obeyed.

What can peasants do against well-trained soldiers? I think I will not see that man of mine again.

Listen. Listen. A clash of steel at the shore. The army of William St Clair is forming in ranks.

THORA   Curse them. Curse the men in high places who will not leave poor folk alone. What harm do we do to anyone? We plough. We reap. We go to the fishing. We pay our heavy taxes. We are peaceful folk.

Once in every generation soldiers march through the green corn. The thatch is set on fire. Soldiers rifle kirn and cupboard. Curse them.

The red wheel begins to turn once more.

There isn't a more peaceful man than my Harald. He has gone into the hills silent as a hawk. He has taken peaceful things with him – scythe and flail – to be things of war.

RAGNA   Oh, I saw them. Indeed I did. And I spoke to them too. I spoke to the highest one of all, William St Clair, the lord William. The Orphir folk had all taken to the hills, men and women and beasts. 'Well,' says I to myself, 'I'm not shifting from the door. What can they want with an old body like me? Even if they do take me and kill me,' says I, 'they're welcome. Life isn't all that pleasant with aches in every limb and my blurred sight. It's all the same to me,' says I, 'what the soldiers do. . . .' So I sat in the doorway in the sun, spinning. It was bright and peaceful. The folk had gone into the hills. I was alone, spinning, in the croft door. Then I heard this fine courteous word in my ear: 'Well, now, grannie, why is everything so quiet in Orphir today? Don't be afraid, grannie, I won't touch a hair of your head. I'm the lord William St Clair. But I'm anxious to know from a wise old mouth how this day will go. See, here's a shilling for you. Tell me something good.' I opened my mouth. I told his lordship a thing or two. It's not for nothing they call me a witch in these parts.

ANNA   I don't belong here at all. I am not an island woman. My home was in Caithness. Why did I ever leave Caithness to live in these Norsky islands? Because I had a child, a boy, that had no father. I came here to be away from sneers and insults.

I have little to do with the other women. They are not my

people. But the soldiers who have landed *are* my people. I will go out and meet them. Perhaps I'll see a known face here and there.

I work hard in the big farm down at the shore. My young son, Angus, he herds the cattle. He is all red hair, freckles, a laughing mouth.

Perhaps the father of Angus will be in the host. That's a brave clash of steel on the road above the shore. It moves now, the clang and the clash, towards the hills.

INGERD   Magnus, be strength and courage in your arm this day, when you go out against those beasts from Scotland! Listen to them now, listen to their Scottish song among the hills. This is the latest of many a Scottish coming. They came in my grandfather's time. 'See,' they said, 'the islands are Scottish, not Norse. The king in the east is too far away. We will trade with you in new Scottish coins. . . .' The Scots came among us. Soon they were in the high places. We (children of Vikings and scholars and discoverers) were the servants and the menials. And they said, 'You will speak the Scots tongue, so we can understand you.' And again, 'Your Norse laws are old and crude. There is a new law book – Scots law – in the castle in Kirkwall. . . .' They said, 'Now you have a Scottish king, King James. Orkney is a true part of the kingdom. . . .' Magnus, son of Norwegians and freemen, show them small mercy, up among the hills, though you have only stones to fling against their foreign steel.

[2]

(*It is noon the same day*)

GUNNHILD   Harder to be a woman, and wait, than to be out there among the flashings and the thunders. The battle has not started yet. They are seeking each other out, the bright army and the shadowy rebels. This is the worst moment. Soon, on the far side of the hill, there will be a wild joyous chorus. For us women here, silent anguish.

Sven, did you say your prayers well last night, and again this morning?

What can the likes of you do, Sven, against William St Clair and the King?

SOLVEIG   The drum stopped beating five minutes ago. This is the worst time. Listen.

Listen. A terrible silence in the hills.

And tomorrow there will be a worse silence. I will sit there at first light in my cottage. My three children will be sleeping. Perhaps I'll be lighting a fire when the knock comes at the door. A helmeted soldier stands there. He will say in a cold voice, 'Woman, the traitor who ploughed this field, Erling, he is a captive of the King. He was taken in battle. He is to be hanged in Kirkwall at noon. You are invited to the ceremony. . . .'

I will say then to the stirring children, 'Lie long. You are the orphans of a traitor. . . .' The innocents, they will not know the meaning of the words.

Listen. Was that a cry on the moor?

THORA   So it falls. Each generation the best ones are taken. They drown in the sea. They lie dead under a castle. They are cut to pieces like beasts in a slaughterhouse.

This is what is done, in the name of glory, to peaceful plough-men and fishermen.

This is glory: to gather sheaves into a barn at the end of harvest. This is glory, to empty a full net into baskets at the shore. This is glory for a man: to sit in peace with his children at home, to break bread under a winter lamp.

I heard a scream and a shout then from the far side of the hill! The other women are turning their heads. Listen.

That blasphemy of fire and sword – that is not glory for a man.

RAGNA   I'm deaf, too. Is it the noise of battle they hear? Why have the women turned their strained faces all one way, like flowers into a black sun? I said to William St Clair, 'Choose one of my balls of wool – one for Caithness, one for Orkney – unroll them – the first thread to finish will lose the battle today. . . .' Smiling, his lordship chose the red ball, for Caithness and the king. I stood up. I unrolled the wool. And the red thread ran out first. . . . His lordship flushed. His lordship took a sovereign out of his purse. He whispered, 'Give me a good omen now, grannie.' I took the gold. I said, 'The first man to fall in battle today, that side will be defeated.' The soldiers seized a herd-boy sitting on a wall. They killed him. Then the soldiers gave a great shout, as if the victory was theirs already.

They marched away.

Soon there was nobody in Orphir but me and the herd-boy with red hair and freckles. He lay there in the ditch. His laughing mouth was a stiff stone.

Terrible things get done. I can hear nothing. Who wins and who loses is not in their hands, the fools.

ANNA   What do I know what these women are thinking? Traitorous things, no doubt. I don't know what they are thinking. I do not belong to them, or to this place.

Listen, the ringing of an axe! And again. The whirr and flight of arrows! Listen. Dull thud of stones on heather and bog and bone. Listen. And cries like dark and bright threads through a tapestry.

I left the women brooding here an hour ago. Like a bird I went to the far side of the hill. I stood on the roadside. The ranked host of lord William came marching, with music, between the hills. I cried aloud, 'Welcome, Caithness men! Honour and success to you this day! I'm a Caithness woman. Some of you will remember me, Anna from Lybster. I bore a son, a fine boy, ten years ago. He herds Smoogroo's cattle in a field a mile back! Did you not see him? He is all red hair, freckles, and a laughing face. . . .' Why, at such blessing from a woman's mouth, did they turn and stare with terror at one another? Even the bonny face of William St Clair turned gray as ashes. They clanged on past me, a stricken army. They marched, a troop of ringing ghosts, for the throat of the valley.

The noise of men and weapons is louder now. The cup of the hills is beginning to brim over with shouts.

I am glad that my young son is not in the mills of war today.

INGERD   Triumph and terror among the hills of Stenness.

Victory *must* be ours. There is no other way. There are such things as justice, truth, honour. Our men cannot lose.

If it had not been for this day, Magnus my son would have lived and died a crofter. A poor man among little stony fields. Magnus will be a hero from this day. I thought we were long past the time of sagas and vikings. I am glad I have lived to see this day.

It can't be otherwise. Listen – I never thought the world could hold such rage and terror. Surely they can hear this battle in Greenland and Denmark. It can't be otherwise. The men of Orkney were scattering castles, they were sailing furthest seas, when the Scots were rooting like swine in bogs.

It is difficult to know Scottish cries from Norse cries. Listen. The hill rings like a mad harp.

Even if my son does not come home, he will be a name in a great story.

[3]

(*It is sunset the same day. The battle is over*)

GUNNHILD   The battle was over. I left this place once the sun was down. How could I find the body of Sven among the red and gray corpses? I went home. In the morning I would take the body from the birds and beasts. I would carry it home. I would send for the priest. A candle would be lit at the head and at the feet of Sven.

When I came to the ridge, there was our house bright at window and open door! Sven, that peaceable man, sat at the fire. He had maps of blood on him. He smiled. He showed me a piece of Caithness silver.

He kissed me, a thing that hasn't happened for twelve years past.

SOLVEIG The battle was over. I lingered here awhile. Summerdale was silent. Many feet moved here and there in the first darkness.

My feet took me homewards. The shadows of the victors drifted here and there; seeking spoils, looking for more blood.

I came to the dark corner of the barn. A tall shadow stood there. I went on my knees. I said, 'I'm not a traitor. I am loyal to the King of Scotland. My husband is Erling, he fought in the battle today, and he's dead. Have pity on me.'

It was a known hand that lay on my head. Erling said, 'You're a foolish woman. We won. Blow up the fire. Put on the pot. The fighting has made me hungry.'

THORA The battle was over. I turned for home. 'Well,' I said, 'I'm a poor woman from now on. No man, not a ha'penny for rent and taxes. The red wheel of war has gone over us. Harald dug this croft out of barren hill twenty years ago. The red wheel of war has gone over the quoy – it is broken. . . .' I said, going home under the barbed stars, 'I have come to a place where grief may be beautiful.' Throngs of shadows moved here and there. A shadow came alongside me. The voice of Harald said, 'Woman, is that you? What are you crying for? You should be dancing till the sun gets up. Orkney has won.'

RAGNA The battle was over. The fools – nothing on earth is

worth all that stir and commotion. I hobbled home through the darkness. Here and there I passed shadows – ploughman, shepherd, boatman – they carried plundered helmets and swords. They laughed like fools to each other under the stars. At the big farm, round the fire, it was all boasting and bragging – 'We broke them with stones! The King's army – every man is dead! We did it, we did it!' The fools – it was the spell of an old woman at the door of death that won the victory this day. They spread out green Caithness coats, tarnished swords. The spoils of battle. St Clair's shilling, and his sovereign – I said nothing about them – I kept them in my purse. I said nothing. I went to my bed. When I got up again they were still at their dancing and drinking in Orphir. The fools!

ANNA   The battle was over. I thought, 'There will be rejoicing down at the shore – the Caithness men lighting victory fires at the cave mouths. There'll be fiddles, eating and drinking. Life is never so sweet as when men have stared at the skull, and lived. There will be kissing at the shore of Orphir tonight. . . .' The night was a host of shadows: shadows with merry Orkney voices. Down beside the Caithness ships at the shore, silence. When I got home, silence. Where was my boy Angus – flame of hair, freckles, laughter? I lit a candle. I looked in the mirror. A skull stared back at me!

INGERD   The battle was over. I stumbled home through rut and bog. The beasts from across the Pentland Firth would be at their plundering soon. Not here, at Quoys. That would pay dear to enter the croft of Quoys! I shuttered stable, byre, barn. The hill was astir all night – ghosts of the slaughtered Orkney boys drifting home – Caithness men prowling here and there, picking, probing. They would not soil this threshold. I had no weapon, nothing. I filled a woollen stocking with stones. I hid behind the peatstack. Just before dawn the first shadow came, a beast,

the King's man. He peered in at the window. He called. He
knocked. The sun got up. He was wearing the green coat and
hat of Caithness. I came behind him. I struck him on the head
with the stocking. And again. Blood gushed from his mouth. He
fell. I turned his head into the sun. The face of Mansie my son
flashed back at me. He was the only Orkney man who died that
day. It will be told in a story next winter.

Silence.
Then a trumpet, and the voice of the unseen herald:
'King James the Fifth of Scotland, to his well-beloved the
people of Orkney. Know that his majesty intends soon to come
among you, bearing the dove of peace: so that all ancient wounds
may be bound up; and that the King's majesty and the lords and
people of Orkney be bound together in a common loyalty
and love.

'God save the King!'

THE LOST BOY

There was one light in the village on Christmas Eve; it came from Jock Scabra's cottage, and he was the awkwardest old man that had ever lived in our village or in the island, or in the whole of Orkney.

I was feeling very wretched and very ill-natured myself that evening. My Aunty Belle had just been explaining to me after tea that Santa Claus, if he did exist, was a spirit that moved people's hearts to generosity and goodwill; no more or less.

Gone was my fat apple-cheeked red-coated friend of the past ten winters. Scattered were the reindeer, broken the sledge that had beaten such a marvellous path through the constellations and the Merry Dancers, while all the children of Orkney slept. Those merry perilous descents down the lum, Yule eve by Yule eve, with the sack of toys and books, games and chocolate boxes, had never really taken place at all. . . . I looked over towards our hearth, after my aunt had finished speaking: the magic had left it, it was only a place of peat flames and peat smoke.

I can't tell you how angry I was, the more I thought about it. How deceitful, how cruel, grown-ups were! They had exiled my dear old friend, Santa Claus, to eternal oblivion. The gifts I would find in my stocking next morning would have issued from Aunty Belle's 'spirit of generosity'. It was not the same thing at all. (Most of the year I saw little enough of that spirit of generosity – at Halloween, for example, she had boxed my ears till I saw stars that had never been in the sky, for stealing a few apples and nuts out of the cupboard, before 'dooking' time.)

If there was a more ill-tempered person than my Aunty Belle

in the village, it was, as I said, old Jock Scabra, the fisherman with a silver ring in his ear and a fierce one-eyed tom cat.

His house, alone in the village, was lit that night. I saw it, from our front door, at eleven o'clock.

Aunty Belle's piece of common sense had so angered me, that I was in a state of rebellion and recklessness. No, I would *not* sleep. I would not even stay in a house from which Santa had been banished. I felt utterly betrayed and bereaved.

When, about half past ten, I heard rending snores coming from Aunty Belle's bedroom, I got out of bed stealthily and put my cold clothes on, and unlatched the front door and went outside. The whole house had betrayed me – well, I intended to be out of the treacherous house when the magic hour of midnight struck.

The road through the village was deep in snow, dark except where under old Scabra's window the lamplight had stained it an orange colour. The snow shadows were blue under his walls. The stars were like sharp nails. Even though I had wrapped my scarf twice round my neck, I shivered in the bitter night.

Where could I go? The light in the old villain's window was entrancing – I fluttered towards it like a moth. How would such a sour old creature be celebrating Christmas Eve? Thinking black thoughts, beside his embers, stroking his wicked one-eyed cat.

The snow crashed like thin fragile glass under my feet.

I stood at last outside the fisherman's window. I looked in.

What I saw was astonishing beyond ghosts or trows.

There was no crotchety old man inside, no one-eyed cat, no ingrained filth and hung cobwebs. The paraffin lamp threw a circle of soft light, and all that was gathered inside that radiance was clean and pristine: the cups and plates on the dresser, the clock and ship-in-the-bottle and tea-caddies on the mantel-piece, the framed picture of Queen Victoria on the wall, the blue stones of the floor, the wood and straw of the fireside chair, the patchwork quilt on the bed.

A boy I had never seen before was sitting at the table. He might have been about my own age, and his head was a mass of bronze ringlets. On the table in front of him were an apple, an orange, a little sailing ship crudely cut from wood, with linen sails, probably cut from an old shirt. The boy – whoever he was – considered those objects with the utmost gravity. Once he put out his finger and touched the hull of the toy ship; as if it was so precious it had to be treated with special delicacy, lest it broke like a soap-bubble. I couldn't see the boy's face – only his bright hair, his lissom neck, and the gravity and joy that informed all his gestures. These were his meagre Christmas presents; silently he rejoiced in them.

Beyond the circle of lamp-light, were there other dwellers in the house? There may have been hidden breath in the darkened box bed in the corner.

I don't know how long I stood in the bitter night outside. My hands were trembling. I looked down at them – they were blue with cold.

Then suddenly, for a second, the boy inside the house turned his face to the window. Perhaps he had heard the tiny splinter-ings of snow under my boots, or my quickened heart-beats.

The face that looked at me was Jock Scabra's, but Jock Scabra's from far back at the pure source of his life, sixty winters ago, before the ring was in his ear and before bad temper and perversity had grained black lines and furrows into his face. It was as if a cloth had been taken to a tarnished web-clogged mirror.

The boy turned back, smiling, to his Christmas hoard.

I turned and went home. I lifted the latch quietly, not to awaken Aunty Belle – for, if she knew what I had been up to that midnight, there would have been little of her 'spirit of genero-sity' for me. I crept, trembling, into bed.

When I woke up on Christmas morning, the 'spirit of the season' had loaded my stocking and the chair beside the bed with boxes of sweets, a Guinness Book of Records, a digital watch, a game of space wars, a cowboy hat, and a 50 pence piece. Aunty Belle stood at my bedroom door, smiling. And, 'A merry Christmas,' she said.

Breakfast over, I couldn't wait to get back to the Scabra house. The village was taken over by children with apples, snowballs, laughter as bright as bells.

I peered in at the window. All was as it had been. The piratical old man sluiced the last of his breakfast tea down his throat from a cracked saucer. He fell to picking his black-and-yellow teeth with a kipper-bone. His house was like a midden.

The one-eyed cat yawned wickedly beside the new flames in the hearth.

MEN AND GOLD AND BREAD

[1]

That peat bank was exhausted, that his great-grandfather had first opened to the sun a hundred years before.

He put his spade into an untouched piece of the hill. He stripped the heather roots off. He dug into wet bog.

He lifted squares of heavy peat and spread them all morning.

He ate bannock and cheese, and drank a bottle of milk, at noon.

He went back to the new-opened bank. He sank his spade. At once his spade rang like a bell.

[2]

What he discovered was an iron-bound box, buried three feet deep.

He smashed the lock with a stone. The chest was full of silver and gold vessels, and rings with heavy cut stones on them, and a scattering of coins.

He thought – 'Now I'm the richest man in the islands. I'm richer than the laird! No more peats – I'll burn coal in a big new house, in five or six fires at the same time. I won't need to plough or fish again.'

He plunged his hands into the gold and silver pieces, as if he was washing them in deathless waters. The goblets and bracelets clashed.

Then he closed the lid of the chest. He sat on it for a long time, and thought.

The sun hung over the western sea.

Far off, other peat cutters were moving home.

The man opened the chest. He took out one golden coin and put it in his pocket. Then he laid the hoard back in the earth and covered the chest up.

He had cut and spread only thirty peats, a poor day's performance.

[3]

The man left the island at midsummer, without a word.

At once his croft and boat began to wither. His thirty cut peats shrivelled on the hillside.

The laird confiscated his cow and pig, in lieu of rent.

Days, months, years passed. A whole generation gathered and broke like a wave on the shore.

The man's croft was a ruin at last.

The crofter never came back.

[4]

The old laird died. His son gathered all the islanders together in the yard of the big house after harvest.

The new laird said, 'I am angry. I am disappointed with you all. I try to show you new ways of agriculture, that will benefit the whole island. But no – you will stick to your old ignorant ways. Listen, you oxen. There's new stirrings in the world. I don't want your rent of stinking butter and rancid ham and the red peats that smoulder into hot ash instead of burning. I want, henceforth, your rents in cash.

'That means you will till the soil of the island in future as my factor, a wise farmer from Aberdeenshire, instructs you.

'My island will be a production machine in future, not a few rags and patches of tilth. My island – our island – will wear a green and yellow coat and it will have a pocket in it, a pocket jingling with coins after every harvest.

'That little annual treasure will be the marvellous result of your sweat and toil throughout the year.

'You will pay me in shillings and guineas for your buildings and fields in future. . . .'

The islanders looked at each other like bewildered oxen. (Silver and gold were things in stories, legends, and songs.)

The men muttered darkly.

The young laird went on, 'You will do as I say. Or I pack every last family of you to Canada and New Zealand. The crofts you have lived in for generations will fall into ruin. I will import sheep, it will be a sheep island, I will get a cash return from the fleeces and mutton, I assure you. Your crofts will be as desolate as that ruin down there at the shore.'

The laird pointed to the ruckle of stones that had been abandoned so long ago by the cutter of thirty peats.

At the end of the day, the islanders agreed to yield their miserable independence and work the whole island estate according to the plans of the new factor.

[5]

One day next spring a boy saw smoke coming from the roof of the ruin to which the young laird had pointed on that day of change after last harvest.

' The boy approached.

Inside the house, on a stone, sat the tramp who had arrived in the island in mid-winter and begged a piece of bread or a cup of milk round the crofts.

The tramp was always so cheerful, in sun or storm, that nearly always he was given something.

And here he sat, in the ruin, at a fire of the most shrivelled peats that the boy had ever seen. The peats on the floor seemed more like bits of rotten cork than the dark rich squares of fire that the wind dried on the hill each summer.

But what amazed the boy utterly was that every niche of the ruin was loaded with gold and silver things – cups, a bowl, candle sticks, jewelled boxes. Six of the old man's fingers shone with rings.

The old man was chuckling to himself. He poured out a flagon of ale he had got from Liza of the Bu into a golden cup, and took deep gulps.

On a broad silver plate lay the two dried cuithes he had begged from the boatman's widow.

The old tramp saw the boy standing in the door.

'Come in, boy,' he said. 'I'm pleased to see you. And who are you, for a boy? Tom of Nessgar was your father, I think. I knew your grandfather, Andrew of Nessgar. You have his eyes and his mouth. A good man. Dead, is he?

'Well boy, you see what a poor place I live in. A poor sty, a poor hovel.

'But I'm not so poor I can't welcome a visitor in the old ways.

'Look, boy, I can't give you much in the way of meat or drink. But take this, take this. Money – that's all that matters in the world nowadays.'

He reached into his rags and took out a large gold coin.

'That's for you, boy,' said the tramp. Take it. The laird, for all his talk of money, doesn't have the like of that doubloon.'

[6]

When a crowd of islanders – men, women and children, led by the boy with the tight golden fist – arrived at the ruin, it was utterly empty.

The treasure that had lined its walls had, it seemed, melted like dew.

There was no sign of the merry old vagrant who had claimed to know Andrew of Nessgar, the boy's grandfather. (How could he have?)

'That boy's a liar,' said Liza of the Bu. 'That boy deserves a good thrashing.'

But there was a glow still at the heart of the peat-dust in the hearth.

The boy's fist opened.

There lay the golden coin that had come back to the island, after measuring in many a city and many a great house and ghetto and desert and island, the vain things of this world.

DARKNESS AND LIGHT

Hogmanay – what did it bring but wind, and rain, and after dark whirls of snow that melted as soon as it fell, except in certain sheltered places and in folds of the hills? And then, towards midnight, rain again, long wind-spun drenching ropes of wetness.

There was no light in Ben's house above the shore. Most likely he had gone to bed. What had Ben to rejoice about? Sanna had been in the kirkyard since early November. Mockery it had been after all, twelve months ago, when the first-footers stood about Ben and Sanna's fire and said, in their dark and bright hogmanay voices, 'Happy New Year!' . . . 'Health and prosperity to Ben and Sanna!' Then the mingled tinklings of glass and pouring whisky.

Early on New Year morning the coat of rain was torn from the island sky. A few stars appeared, in the north and the west. The road glittered here and there with pool-stars, ditch-stars, stone-stars. A voice sounded from this house and that: figures appeared in doorways, shrugging into coats, the doorways were rich lighted rectangles in the solid block of this farm, that croft. Torches flickered and beamed: shadows trooped into one company of hearty shadows at the end of a road. More and more stars enriched the sky. They were bright enough, the stars, to put a gleam on tilted bottles, to invest a winter ditch with minute jewellery.

'Where'll we go first?' came a voice from the troop of shadows.

'To Crufdale, of course,' came the response (a high heroic voice). 'To Ben's and Sanna's.'

This was followed by a brief silence, a shuffling of feet. Someone coughed.

'To Ben's,' said a low voice. 'We'll go to Ben's now. . . .'

At Crufdale the door was locked. The place was in blackness, or almost in blackness: when Tommy put his forge-red face against the window, there was a glow in the grate. In the deep chair beside the grate sat Ben. Ben's eyes shone in a sudden flare and gulp of flame from the banked fire.

'Ben, it's us!' cried Tommy. 'Let's in, Ben.'

Other voices were at the window then; other breath, that stained the glass so that Ben was a glimmering ghost inside. 'A Happy New Year, Ben!' And, 'Open up, Ben! We've got some good malt here.' And, 'Are you all right, Ben?'

Ben paid no more attention than if they had been shadows indeed, and voiceless shadows.

'A queer old thing!' said Sander when five fruitless minutes of cajolery and raillery had passed. 'I always told you, he would break up if anything happened to Sanna.'

'It was Sanna we always came to see,' said Geoff. 'Sanna was the cheery one.'

'A queer way to start the year!' said Bilton beside the peat-stack. 'Turned away from the first door – an unlucky thing, that!'

From the gate Tommy called back. 'A good year anyway, Ben! May it be a better year for you than the one that's just past.'

They exchanged bottles on the road outside. They heard other revellers a mile away, coming along the hill road: a chorus, a high wild sudden 'yarroo!' as if a Cherokee had been enrolled in their company.

The rejected first-footers set off to the hamlet that straggled along the shore a mile to the north, a scatter of bright and dark windows.

The night put on its rain-coat again and the dozen companies of first-footers were soaked, all over the island. To some the rain was a delicious sky-essence dripping from their noses, breaking up their vision comically, filling the road with beautiful brimming mirrors that their feet smashed uncertainly through, time and again. To others the rain was the last twist in their rack of misery. It rained from four o'clock in the morning till after six, a wind-wavering downpour, a lustration upon the door-step of the new year. Then the rain-coat was torn again, and the first star shone through.

In the last of the rain Amos came to Ben's door. His pocket bulged with a dark load. He lifted the latch and pushed. The door rattled but remained fast.

'Ben!' shouted Amos. 'Are you in your bed, man? It's me, Amos.' The house was silent as a stone.

Amos took his face to the window. There, over the fire-glow, crouched Ben. Amos knocked sharply on the pane. Ben didn't let on to hear. As Amos watched, Ben took a cup from the hearth and put the rim to his mouth and tilted it. Whisky gives the face of the drinker a different expression from tea or ale or water.

'Ben,' shouted Amos, and knocked again.

At a distant farm a dog barked wildly, and was as suddenly silent. Another household was receiving those who carried the New Year blessing.

And now Amos saw that Ben was speaking and probably speaking to him; for the eyes of the old boatman were fixed on him. The mouth moved, the old hands gesticulated a little, the head nodded gently from time to time.

'I can't hear you, man,' shouted Amos. 'Let me in! I thought you might be lonely. That's why I came.'

It seemed to Amos that Ben smiled from time to time. But he made no move to stir from armchair to door, to let his oldest friend in. He opened his palm in Amos's direction, his mouth moved, his eyes crinkled again. There was a brief silence; he shook his head; then he resumed the inaudible monologue.

Amos brought the whisky bottle out of his pocket and held it up. That might be the key that would let him in. It turned out not to be. Through the glass Ben continued to talk to Amos, mildly and reasonably.

Nothing is more infuriating than a seen language that is incomprehensible: a cry under water, a shout into a gale. What was the one old man trying to tell the other? Maybe that this Hogmanay business was a lot of nonsense – hordes of young drunken yahoos – their last year's greetings and kissings hadn't done Sanna much good. . . . He could have been saying, on the other hand, that the rowan tree at the end of the house had been loaded with berries and so it was likely to be a hard winter; he hoped Amos has plenty of peats in his stack.

Was he trying to tell Amos that a letter had come at last from young Ben in Alberta. But there was nothing of importance in the letter, the usual items of getting and spending – nothing important enough, at any rate, to make him rise from his comfortable chair.

It was possible that Ben was speaking about Sanna. It seemed likely, indeed, from the frequent smiles that dimpled the soliloquy. They had been as happy together, give and take a few fights, rows, sulks and silences, as any couple in the island. He was telling Amos maybe that yes – it was lonely now without Sanna. Why on earth was Sanna taken and Ben left that could do hardly a thing for himself? (The district nurse had to see to him once a week. The home-help came weekly, too, to clean up his dust and bruck.)

Could Ben be saying – what was true – that Amos had courted Sanna the summer before Ben himself had appeared on the scene, newly home from sea after a year's sailing? Though Ben had married Sanna the next spring, for some reason Ben had always seemed to be jealous that Amos had got the first of Sanna's kisses; and for that reason, it could be, he wasn't letting Amos in on this particular night. Let him bide out there in the darkness and the rain. It was Sanna Amos had always really

come to see at New Year. Why couldn't he go down to the kirkyard and talk to Sanna there?

That, thought Amos (his hands and eyes soaked with another
blind shower) would be a likely thing for Ben to say. He might
indeed visit Sanna in the kirkyard before going home to his
porridge and tea.

Amos, stone deaf in the last of the rain and the darkness,
shook his head and stamped his feet. Once he opened his bottle
and threw his head back and let his Adam's apple wobble. He
sprinkled a few drops of whisky over the window-sill. 'A good
year to this house anyway,' he said.

Inside, Ben poked the fire. He took another small sip out of
the cup on the hearth. He turned to the patient man at the
window; smiling; nodding; crinkling his eyes; moving his
mouth into a hundred shapes.

It could have been great wisdom or great poetry, though that
was unlikely, coming from Ben.

'I expect,' thought Amos, 'he's wishing me luck, among other
things, with the croft this coming year – a good sowing and
harvest. He's a kind man, Ben, though he was always a bit lazy
himself, as far as the fishing went. Sanna didn't exactly live like
a duchess.'

When Amos, after his solitary toast and blessing, turned to
go home, the winter sun was just rising in the south-east. The
new light brightened his forehead. Behind him, Ben's window
flashed and flamed.